ABOUT THE AUTHOR

As a science graduate, part-time university lecturer and experienced secondary school teacher, Karen J. Jones enjoys sharing her passion for science with a wide audience. She is a Chartered Scientist, as well as a Chartered Chemist, and has studied Creative Writing and Linguistics at degree level.

Her natural enthusiasm to teach science flows effortlessly through her writing; engaging her readers on a journey of scientific discovery. She has received excellent Ofsted feedback for her innovative approach to teaching 'Murder Science' (Forensic Science) to mixed age-groups of children during school extra-curricular sessions.

Karen has had one non-fiction book published, *Competitive Edge – Prize Winning Secrets*, and is planning to release poetry and short story collections in the near future.

DECEPTIVE ENCOUNTERS

Karen J. Jones

Matador
9 De Montfort Mews
Leicester LE1 7FW, UK
Tel: (+44) 116 255 9311 / 9312
Email: books@troubador.co.uk
Web: www.troubador.co.uk/matador

ISBN 978 1848760 493

Disclaimer: all names, characters, places and incidents detailed in
Deceptive Encounters are products of the author's imagination or are
used fictitiously. Any resemblance to actual events or persons, living
or dead, is entirely coincidental.

Typeset in 11pt Stempel Garamond by Troubador Publishing Ltd, Leicester, UK
Printed in the UK by TJ International Ltd, Padstow, Cornwall

Matador is an imprint of Troubador Publishing Ltd

For my son, Alex, whose vivid imagination has contributed to the more gory aspects of the crime scene scenarios, and to my friends and family for their support.

INTRODUCTION

Each chapter of *Deceptive Encounters* introduces scientific concepts which support Key Stages two (KS2) and three (KS3) of the National Curriculum for Science. Readers are guided through carefully structured scenarios which link the scientific disciplines of Forensic Science, Biology, Chemistry, Physics and Geology. Learning is unavoidable as the reader subconsciously links scientific concepts and details in an attempt to solve the case.

It is envisaged that as well as serving as a forensic science novel for secondary and upper-primary school-aged readers, 'Deceptive Encounters' can be used as a cross-curricular fiction novel, for use in KS2 and KS3 Science, English and Geography lessons.

A glossary of the scientific terms used within this novel is included.

CHAPTER ONE

Lauren sang quietly to herself whilst dancing along to 'footloose' blaring from the kitchen radio, before attempting to squeeze her packed-lunch into her already bulging rucksack. She had an uncharacteristic enthusiasm to head off to school this morning. At just past eight o'clock, and with a brisk ten minute walk to her destination, she would arrive forty minutes earlier than necessary.

Her twin sister, Robyn, had woken late and was still showering, not fully aware of the plans that were being hatched. She hoped to persuade her mum, Elizabeth Bale, to drop her off at school at half past eight, whilst on her way to work at Chase-Brooke solicitors in the neighbouring hamlet of Lychford Green.

As Elizabeth heard the front door open she called out to her daughter, "Bye, Lauren, don't forget to phone me from Emma's tonight, just to let me know you're alright. I'll see you tomorrow after school."

"Don't worry mum, I haven't let you down yet have I? I'll phone sometime after eight, when we're all outside for the barbeque," replied Lauren. She was astounded that both girls' mothers trusted them to such an extent that they hadn't felt the need to cross-check the information they had been given; the barbeque detail being only partially true, mentioned to give a hint of authenticity.

Lauren and Emma had practiced writing invitations in their respective mother's handwriting to perfection over recent weeks; both dreading the consequences of their elaborate plans being foiled.

As Lauren turned the corner from Gracemere Close into Allen Mead Lane, her pace quickened, as if matching her elevated heartbeat. Excitement mingled with apprehension and the guilt of deceit as she caught a glimpse of Jamie Jackson heading towards the large metal school gates. She desperately tried to fight off the tears that were welling at the thought of having lied to her mother before she left home earlier. "It's too late to change anything now," she thought to herself, as she summoned the strength to appear brave and carefree like her street-wise friend, Emma.

Lauren silently approached her two friends who were waiting on the large well-worn marble stairs outside of the school library; they had just a few minutes before the 8.50am registration-bell to finalise the day's details.

The two girls intended to bunk off school at the end of lunch break, just before their Drama and Music lessons, and to return just in time to meet the afternoon registration at 3.45pm. They reckoned that their teachers wouldn't detect their absence, especially old Mr Heath from the Drama department, who referred to Emma by a different name each lesson. They would head back to the beach after school to meet up with Jamie by the barbeque area, where they would eat their sandwiches and stay until the early hours of the morning; innocently gazing up at the stars, tracking satellites across the night-sky, and perhaps taking a swim or going snorkelling in the sea by moonlight.

Jamie's parents were away overnight, attending a convention; his father, Dr. Mark Jackson, was presenting a paper on his research of the many Jurassic fossils discovered along the local coastline. Jamie had often been left alone at home before, with responsibility to look after their elderly Alsatian dog, Sooty; childminders having long-since been abandoned, owing to his determination to insult and humiliate them at every opportunity.

The three friends had become inseparable since they met at junior school in year two (five years ago) and, though not now in the same form classes at the newly-built Allen Mead Secondary School in Longbarrow, they met almost daily after classes and during most evenings, often accompanied by Lauren's identical twin sister, Robyn.

On this occasion, Robyn wasn't invited, as she couldn't be relied upon to keep the plot a secret from their mother. It was imperative that she should not suspect anything unusual either at school, or on the way home. On this count, Jamie had called in a favour, and had arranged for Robyn's dishy new Australian friend, Brett, a cousin to Lauren's closest-friend, Samantha Stryder, (who was presently at home with chickenpox), to wait for her after school, outside of the school gate, and then offer to take her to the cinema.

After painting and firing a ceramic tile in the art studio, and then looking at the cellular structure of Spirogyra with light-microscopes in the Biology laboratory, the much-awaited lunch bell sounded. The half-hour break would present the perfect opportunity for Lauren to mingle with as many friends as possible whilst eating her sandwiches, and then to assist Emma, who planned to feign an asthma attack whilst waiting in the hot-food queue. They hoped that their memorable, highly visibile actions in the canteen would provide them with an alibi; using the medical room as a possible explanation for their location if their absence was noticed during the afternoon lessons.

As the of end-of-lunch bell resonated throughout the building, the time finally arrived for them to gracefully slip away from site and embark on the covert adventure that had been painstakingly planned. They sidled discretely behind the sports centre building, as if vaguely en-route to their next lesson in the drama block and made their escape by crawling through the gap in the school fence, scurrying across the cemetery and then demurely emerging on the pathway adjacent to the brightly-coloured Victorian beach huts (so as not to arouse suspicion from passers-by).

With their hearts pounding almost audibly, and adrenaline surging, both girls were too pre-occupied and nervous to stop and talk; Emma's wheezy-panting revealing her underlying asthmatic breathing complication, for which she refused to administer the inhaler medication that had been prescribed following her collapse in class last month during the first week of the summer term.

Ozone-rich air laced with the obligatory seaside aroma of rotting seaweed, and of freshly-caught fish, (on sale at the trawler owner's hut), gently wafted over the sea wall, softening the effect of the Sun's intense rays beating down on the pristine adolescent skin of the girls' faces.

The beach itself was almost devoid of people, except for a few mothers with pre-school children all of whom appeared intent on building sandcastle fortresses, or tunnelling through the soft creamy-white sand as if trying to link-up with Australia. Herring gulls mingled among the sun bathers, cackling loudly, whilst squabbling over discarded fish innards and jellyfish which had become tangled in the fishing nets.

A solitary police car had parked alongside the wooden beach-side trawler hut; one policeman was scribbling profusely in his notebook, whilst another could be seen taking photographs on the deck of the cordoned-off trawler, which had been hauled up onto the beach into its usual mooring position.

The blaring siren of another police vehicle, approaching in the far distance, quickened in pace and increased in amplitude as it got closer to the tiny resort of Longbarrow.

Lauren was intrigued. She assumed that the boat had been in some kind of accident, or had landed something unusual, such as one of the old WWII anti-boat mines that occasionally got washed ashore. Another possibility could be that one of the large, aggressive local sea-lions had managed to gain access to the trawler's deck, and was helping itself to the fish stock, as occasionally happened. On any other day than today, she would have been more than keen to investigate the matter.

"Just our luck!" Emma exclaimed, whilst turning away from the source of action. "We'd better get out of here quickly before anyone recognises us."

"Let's get rid of our uniforms first," suggested Lauren, "we'll blend in better with the tourists. It's probably best to pretend we haven't noticed them, so we don't attract attention to ourselves."

Emma wasted no time in removing her white school blouse and unzipping her school mini-skirt, teasingly revealing the new dainty lace-effect bikini that she'd bought the previous week. Lauren kicked off her shoes and casually stripped down to her sensibly-styled Speedo school swimming costume, before carefully applying high factor sun-block to protect the easily-burnt pale freckled-skin of her shoulders.

"Let's head around the corner to the cove – there won't be much chance of anyone finding us there," said Lauren, excitedly, before racing down the concrete steps onto the hot pebble-strewn sand, toward the cooler more-compact surface at the water's edge.

Emma had long-since yearned to try topless bathing, to feel the Sun's rays intimately caressing her newly shaped body whilst partially tanning the delicate whiter-

6

areas of skin that the Sun cannot usually reach, however, she didn't feel brave enough to attempt this in front of anyone, not even her best friend Lauren. To overcome the problem she bought herself a 'tan-through' costume, which had cost her considerably more than her pocket money allowed; she had secretly pocketed most of her school lunch money from the previous two weeks to help pay for it; causing her to faint in the hot classrooms twice during mid-afternoon in the last week. She still didn't feel fully recovered.

The grey limestone cliffs surrounding them in the cove sported many joints which trickled with water, glistening in the sunshine. The cliff top and many of the ledges were capped by lush tufted grass and wild flowers, whereas the lower sections of rock all along the tide line were discoloured by dark green fine-textured seaweed interspersed with limpets.

Large rusty signs were attached to boulders which blocked the entrance to the cove from the beach and also onto rock face itself, stating: 'Danger – Do Not Climb! Unstable Rock Structure.'

"Fantastic, there's nobody around here!" Emma exclaimed. "Can you see the gap in the rock over there? That might be the cave that I overheard Jamie talking about last week; apparently it's much bigger inside than it looks from the outside. Let's check it out."

"It doesn't look very safe up there, does it? We'd have to climb with bare feet," replied Lauren. "Wouldn't you rather have a quick swim and do a spot of sunbathing before we head back to school? We can't afford to miss getting back in time for registration."

"Do what you wish. I'm going to investigate the cave to see what all the fuss is about," replied Emma.

"Okay then Emma, if you're really determined to go, then I'll go with you, but please be careful. You saw the warning signs back there didn't you? We can't afford to have any sort of accident; else we'll get into so much trouble. We're both supposed to be in class, remember!"

Despite only having been exposed to the Sun for less than an hour, the two girls had become intensely burned. Lauren's freckled face, shoulders, legs and arms took on a red, cooked-lobster appearance; this, she thought, would be very difficult to explain back at school later, so she removed a t-shirt from her rucksack and covered her upper body with it. Sunburn had been a lifetime problem for the ginger-haired, pale-skinned child, a genetic trait handed down from her father's side of the family.

Emma's shoulders and forehead were also red and becoming painfully hot. Her concentration was starting to deteriorate, causing her to lose her footing on one of the loose rough-surfaced boulders. She slipped sideways with her left foot, and screamed loudly as she fell onto the jagged rocks in front of her. Her shins, knees and hands were grazed and bleeding, and her foot had already begun to throb. Swelling started to appear around her inflamed ankle joint. As she tried to stand and regain her composure, she fell again, sobbing quietly. "Sorry, Lauren, I can't go any further, I think I've broken my foot," she whimpered, feeling sorry for herself.

"That's just typical!" Lauren replied, unsympathetically. She slowly climbed down the rocks to where her friend was crouched. "I told you to be careful! Let me have a look at it. Can you try wiggling your toes for me? If you can, then it's probably only a sprain."

"What do you mean by 'only' a sprain?" Emma retorted angrily.

"What's the point arguing about it, eh? You'd better think up a really good excuse to explain this to everyone when we get back! Anyway, my mum says that the best thing for a sprained ankle is to soak your foot in cold water, which is supposed to stop the swelling and reduce any bruising – it has got to be worth giving it a go."

Their rucksacks were flung high onto a ledge before the girls plunged into a nearby deep rock pool in an attempt to relieve Emma's painful foot, and to cool both of their hot sunburned bodies.

Lauren couldn't contain her laughter at the sight of Emma relaxing in the pool, revealing a little of more of herself than she ought to.

"Hey, Emma, where did you get that costume from?" Lauren giggled.

"I got it from the new Ann Summers shop in Lychford Green, do you like it?"

"Maybe you should have checked the instructions first, 'cos it's gone completely see-through now that you've got it wet," replied Lauren, sniggering.

"No, you're joking me!" Emma replied, blushing

profusely. She tried desperately to place her hands and arms in strategic positions to cover the unexpectedly-exposed parts of her body. Her embarrassment was obvious; making her vulnerability even funnier for her friend, who was unsuccessfully trying hard to contain her laughter. Emma's blushed-face now merged in well with her sunburn. "I can't be seen like this, not even by you." She checked her watch – it was nearing half past two – and then told Lauren to close her eyes for a minute or two whilst she climbed out of the rock pool and crawled, semi-nakedly, up to the nearby cave entrance to rest and to allow her costume to dry-off. Her bleeding knees and painful ankle seemed insignificant compared with her impromptu nudity.

Lauren did as she was told, and followed on behind Emma a few minutes later. She was temporarily distracted by thoughts of her classmates attempting to syncopate a rhythm in dishy Mr Stevens's lesson; wondering also if her absence from class had been noticed at all.

The cave smelt musty and dank. The back wall trickled with water, echoing as it dripped into the small rivulet which meandered its way along the floor before eventually channelling out through cave mouth as a tiny waterfall. The setting was tranquil.

A pile of tinned-food, cooking utensils, beer, clothing, blankets and personal items neatly stacked to the East side of the cave indicated that the cave had recently been lived in. Lauren jittered at the thought that the cave occupant might return soon. She located an obscured niche for them both to rest in just long enough to dry off their wet clothing; they couldn't return to school without drying off – it would be bad enough with the unexplained sunburn!

The effect of the Sun's intense heat, and the gentle sound of distant waves breaking onto the pebble-strewn beach promoted an overwhelming desire to sleep for a while. Resting with their backs propped up against a large dry boulder, and facing a cooling breeze, they closed their eyes, intending to rest for a few minutes before making their way back to school. It wasn't long before they were both asleep.

Several hours must have passed before Lauren woke to the sound of water lapping up against the cave mouth. It was impossible to see the hands of her watch in the darkness of the cave, which was by now lit faintly by moonlight. She was cold and still damp.

School would have long-since closed, and the tide was now well-in.

She paced around the cave agitated, wondering how long she had been asleep, and then recalling that they had agree to meet up with Jamie after school. "Will he be looking for us, or will he assume we've stood him up? Where are the rucksacks?" She remembered her promise to phone home sometime after eight o'clock, and knew her mum would be sitting at home waiting for her call, and for Robyn to return home from the cinema. "What about Mrs Waldron? Will she be waiting to hear from Emma?" Tears tumbled uncontrollably down her cheeks at the thought of the hopelessness of the situation. She gently roused Emma from her deep slumber by rocking her shoulder.

Within a short while the sea was aglow with light radiating in all directions from a clearly definable source. It was heading directly toward the cave. Underwater rocks, seaweed and fish were swathed in light as the phenomenon intensified. With mouths open, and bodies shaking, Lauren and Emma were both gripped by fear; temporarily unable to scream, shout, or move from where they stood. The cave interior lit as the light source closed-in on the target, the silhouette of a scuba diver now becoming visible. Both girls scrambled back to the security of their hiding place. Lauren's watch face was now visible, the time was 10.35pm.

The scuba diver emerged from the water, dripping onto the floor of the cave entrance, before casually propping a harpoon gun up against the wall. He removed his mask, flippers, oxygen tank, and finally the thick rubber diving suit. These were all then neatly placed next to the pile of personal belongings at the side of the cave. The moonlit backdrop revealed a tall, young, muscular male, with shoulder-length blonde hair, wearing knee-length shorts and a vest-type shirt. He hummed a tune to himself; Elton John's 'Candle in the Wind'. Both girls were familiar with the melody line, as their whole school had been practicing this for an assembly recently.

He lit a small pre-made fire close to the cave mouth, onto which he dropped a couple of freshly filleted fish. The aroma of fish and billowing smoke filled the cave. Emma tried desperately to refrain from coughing by crouching down and holding her breath. A stabbing sensation between the ribs made her scream aloud – a harpoon arrow head had been pressed against her skin.

"Miss Bale and Miss Waldron isn't it? What are you doing here?" Asked the diver, who was now clearly visible, and standing in front of them. He retracted the harpoon before turning his back on them, and returning to his cooking.

"Oh my God, it's Mr Michael, our history teacher," Emma whispered to Lauren, "isn't he just drop-dead-gorgeous? He reminds me of a wingless angel."

Lauren quickly loosened down her ponytail (the only differentiating feature between her and her twin, Robyn), in an attempt to avoid absolute identification, whilst masking her excitement to be alone with the very eligible young, handsome, blonde-haired teacher. "Mr Michael, it's a real surprise to find you here too," she replied, quietly. "We were on our way home from a walk on the beach after school, when Emma slipped and twisted her ankle; she couldn't walk very well on it, so we rested here for a while. We should let her mum know she's okay, I suppose. Do you have a mobile phone we can use? Ours are still in our rucksacks, out there on the rocks somewhere."

"Sorry, Miss Bale, I don't carry one when I'm diving. Mine's back in my car," he replied. "What time are you both due back home?"

"There isn't a definite time, as long as we're not too late. We're supposed to be camping overnight in the garden at Lauren's house. Her mum probably thinks we're in our tent already, so don't worry, she won't be missing us," interjected Emma, "and anyway, you'll be much better company than hedgehogs and slugs."

Lauren turned to Emma and whispered: "What are you playing at?" Emma turned her head away, ignoring the question.

"Is there enough fish there for us too? We're absolutely ravishing!" Emma felt herself blushing beneath her sunburn at her mistaken use of the word, and coyly leant forward so that her long dark brown hair covered most of her face and some of her costume (which had now dried to full opacity).

Lauren glanced at Emma, rolling her eyes briefly in disbelief at her friend's flirtation.

"Girls, it's probably best if you keep quiet about being here with me; this needs to remain a secret," commented Mr Michael. "You are welcome to call me Luke out of school – it sounds a lot less stuffy." The girls smiled at each other, but offered no response.

The two fish provided an adequate meal between three people, washed down by with a mug-full of warm cloudy beer. Both girls felt slightly woozy after their meal, and stifled yawns whilst struggling desperately to stay awake long enough to engage their host in conversation.

"Don't worry girls - sleep it off if you need to. It's been a hot day today, and you've probably been out in the sunshine for too long. Anyway, it will be several hours before the tide is low and safe enough for you to leave here. I'll look out for you."

Lauren wasn't quite sure what was meant by the last remark, and was too tired to ask. She leant against Emma, who had propped herself up against a large, dry, smooth-surfaced rock next to the cave side wall, and closed her eyes.

Luke covered each girl carefully with a blanket from his pile of personal belongings as they slept, prior to donning his wetsuit again and quietly slipping back into the sea, unnoticed.

Emma and Lauren woke to the sound of seagulls at 8am. They had no recollection of events after they had eaten the fish, and were startled to find themselves fully dressed, Emma's ankle neatly bandaged, and their school-bags placed beside them. They were alone.

They clambered out of the cave, across the rocks, and back home to get changed and to grab something to eat before walking back to school. They had to be on-time for the morning registration bell. This had to be timed correctly to avoid meeting their respective parents before they left for work.

Emma caught a glimpse of a tanned blonde-haired man standing in a telephone box outside of the Post Office, on the opposite side of the road, as they hurried past the village shops. The awkward manner with which he held the telephone receiver caught her attention.

CHAPTER TWO

As Lauren changed her clothes, she noticed bruising around her torso and thighs that she didn't remember from the day before. In fact, there were many details that she didn't remember. Surprisingly, the name label inside her blouse was that of another girl, Angela Stoker, who had been missing from home since last week. Lauren thought that she might have mistakenly picked up Angela's blouse from the P.E changing rooms recently, and wondered how Robyn hadn't noticed the name tag when she did the weekly ironing.

Police had interviewed friends and neighbours, whilst regular newspaper bulletins and the local television news had highlighted Angela's plight at every opportunity. The Bale family had been subjected to lengthy questioning on more than one occasion, following a legal restraining order that they had initiated against several members of the Stoker household, earlier in the year.

Despite Lauren's joy at her tormentor's disappearance, she felt she had a duty to report the lost property to school, who would no doubt contact the police on her behalf.

As expected, when she arrived at school, the register showed an unauthorised absence during the last registration of the previous day. Lauren wasted no time in handing a carefully folded note to her form tutor, in what appeared to be her mother's handwriting, belatedly apologising for not informing the school of an urgent dentist appointment the previous day. No questions were asked, much to her relief.

History was the first lesson on the timetable for Tuesday morning. Both girls were nervous and embarrassed at the thought of attending Mr Michael's lesson, as well as having to answer questions from their classmates relating to their missed lessons the previous day. They lingered quietly at the rear of the queue, hoping to blend into the wall. To their relief, Miss Harper opened the door, and ushered everyone into the classroom.

"Good morning class. Mr Michael is not presently in school, so I'll be teaching you today," announced Miss Harper.

"Where is he, Miss?" Robyn asked, disappointedly.

"I must admit that I'm not sure – perhaps he's not well. You can ask him when you next see him," she responded, noting the less than enthusiastic atmosphere in the room. "I will pick up where he left you."

"I doubt that very much!" Emma muttered to herself, blushing profusely at her memories of their last encounter.

By morning break-time, rumours were circulating that a Ford Mondeo car, the same colour as the one Mr Michael owned, had been found at the base of a cliff overlooking the cove at Longbarrow earlier that morning during low-tide. The incident had been reported on the local radio station, which could be heard blaring from the art technicians' preparation area.

Lauren ushered Emma into the girls' toilet block. "There wasn't anything unusual in the sea when we left, was there?" Lauren asked.

"Not where we were, else we would have seen it," she replied.

Lauren lifted her blouse slightly. "Hey, take a look at this bruise, Emma! I can't remember this happening; there are a few others as well. Do you think I should do something about it?"

"Hell – that looks really painful. Where are the others?" Emma asked.

"On my legs, mainly," she replied quietly, whilst looking down at the floor, hoping not to catch Emma's gaze. "You don't think he, ermm, you-know, umm, did something to me when I was asleep do you?"

"It looks a bit odd to me! I think we'd better get you to a doctor straight after school, to check things out, you know, just to be sure. You might need to tell your mum where we're going, 'cos they'll probably phone her from the surgery anyway," Emma replied sympathetically.

"Hmm, I'm not sure – it's all so embarrassing. Just think – he must have dressed us somehow, so who knows what else happened? I'm really scared now," sobbed

Lauren, whilst anxiously rubbing her silver crucifix pendant between her fingers. "My mum will be absolutely furious!"

At that moment the entrance door flung open, as Robyn entered. "Hey, sis, what happened with you yesterday then?" She asked. "You told mum you'd ring her."

"It must have been bad phone reception – I couldn't get through, sorry. I hope she wasn't too annoyed," Lauren replied.

"She tried phoning your mum, Emma, but nobody answered," said Robyn.

"Everyone would have been outside for the barbeque, so she probably didn't hear it ringing," she replied abruptly, as if it was quite a normal occurrence.

"Hmm, really? I'm not sure I believe you," snapped Robyn.

"It's really not that important. I'll text mum to let her know I'm okay," replied Lauren, hoping to avoid any further questions. "Anyway, please tell us how your date with Brett went last night."

"Not quite as planned. You had to be fifteen to see the film, so they wouldn't let me in, even though I had makeup and smartish clothes on. Brett and I walked down to the beach instead, since we had a few hours to spare – it was really quite romantic. We sat on the wall, eating fish and chips, while watching the last rays of the Sun melting into the horizon. He even rested his arm on my shoulder," replied Robyn, smiling, as if in a daydream-like trance.

"Will you both be going out again, then?" Emma asked, trying not to giggle.

Robyn blushed, and pretended not to have heard the question. "I bet you'll never guess who else we saw there!"

"Who?"

"I'll tell you after school," Robyn replied, teasingly, whilst combing her long, silky, ginger hair. "Anyway, we'd better hurry, or we'll be late for our next lesson."

A note in the register summoned Emma and Lauren to the Headteacher's office. To both girls' surprise, Mrs Bale and Ms Waldron were waiting patiently for them in the corridor. Everyone forced a brief smile, acknowledging each others' presence.

"What's happened to your foot, Emma?" Mrs Bale enquired.

Ms Waldron's expression changed rapidly, as she faced the other mother, responding before her daughter had chance to reply to the question. "Emma phoned me this morning to tell me she slipped into the fish pond at your party last night, and that you bandaged her ankle for her. Maybe I'm over-reacting, but I would have expected someone to have contacted me last night, to let me know there'd been an accident, mainly as a matter of courtesy. How can you possibly not remember what happened to her?"

Emma stared at the floor, her body trembling, whilst Lauren fidgeted uneasily on her chair, tears welling in the corners of her eyes.

"How rude! You invited Lauren to your house for the night. I entrusted her to your care, expecting you to supervise them properly. It appears you have not fulfilled this obligation," replied Mrs Bale, who by now was red-faced, standing, and spitting her words.

"I have absolutely no idea what you're talking about!" Replied Ms Waldron, who was now almost shouting.

Both women turned away from each other, unaware that their daughters had already been ushered away.

"Ms Joanna Waldron? Mrs Elizabeth Bale? This way please," directed the Headteacher, as he led the two women along the corridor and into his large multi-functional office. "Do be seated."

There were two other adults, chatting to each other, occupying one of the three large sofas. The two girls sat together, silently, in the centre of another, with just enough space to their side for each parent.

"Thank you both for attending this meeting at such very short notice, ladies. Let me introduce myself and my colleague to you. I am Detective Constable Steve Turner, and this is Crime Scene Investigator, Alexia Stermont," said one of the unknown adults. "We are investigating a missing person report; that of Mr Luke Michael, and have been led to believe that there is information that your daughters may be able to provide, that will assist with our investigation. We are required to offer a child's parents the opportunity to be present when we question any person who is under 16 years of age. Today, we intend to have a general discussion; mainly just to gather information, rather than to conduct a formal interview."

Both girls looked at each other in a state of disbelief.

"Could you please leave us now, Mr Clarke. Thank you for your help so far; we'll be in contact with you again soon," CSI Stermont said to the Headteacher, whilst stepping forward to shake his hand.

"Miss Bale, Miss Waldron, good afternoon," said DC Turner to the two nervous children. "As you might possibly have heard on the local news bulletin today, a car was recovered locally from the base of the cliff this morning at low tide; this has been confirmed as belonging to Mr Michael, who's whereabouts have been undetermined since last Friday evening. The car does not appear to have been occupied at the time of impact."

"What has this got to do with Emma?" Ms Waldron asked the detective.

"Two school books, and a lunch box, possibly belonging to your daughter, have been recovered from the wreckage, Ms Waldron," replied DC Turner.

"He's her history teacher, so he could have her book for marking," replied Ms Waldron, smugly, "anyway, she's always losing her lunch box, which is why she now has school dinners." Emma rummaged through her bag, as her mum spoke, and then turned to look Lauren in the eyes.

"Miss Waldron, are you able to explain why your property was in the car?" DC Turnbull asked.

She looked at him, and shrugged her shoulders.

"CSI Stermont's team is presently subjecting the box, and contents for forensic examination. If your mother is indeed correct, and you do not currently use a lunchbox, then we will require your fingerprints to help eliminate you from our enquiry."

"Sorry mum, sorry Mrs Bale," said Emma, as she focussed her gaze on the floor, "we really should have told you the truth about last night. Lauren and I went to the beach for a while after school yesterday, not to a party like we told you. We were going to have a barbeque there, with our friends. Whilst we were there, I did leave my bag on the rocks for a while. I suppose anyone could have taken my stuff."

Ms Waldron stared at her daughter. "What else is there that you're not telling us then?"

"As you can see, I slipped and twisted my ankle. The tide cut us off, so we couldn't get home safely. I didn't think you would want us to try climbing over slippery rocks, and risk drowning. We couldn't phone you, 'cos our mobiles were in our bags, and we couldn't reach them," replied Emma, nudging Lauren firmly in the ribs with her elbow, whilst directing her answer more to DC Turnbull than her mother. Ms Waldron and Mrs Bale both leant forwards, turned and then stared at each other, by way of acknowledgement following the admission of their daughters' deception.

"Miss Waldron, the register shows that you were absent from school yesterday, all afternoon," added DC Turner, "whereas Miss Bale is marked as having attended a medical appointment."

"The teacher must have made a mistake," snapped Mrs Bale, "Lauren was in school all day. I'm sure my other daughter, Robyn, can confirm that for you."

CSI Stermont looked up from the notepad that she had been writing in. "Miss Bale, I have a question for you. We recovered a bottle of Rohypnol wrapped in an item of your clothing in the car boot, as well as Miss Waldron's books and lunchbox. Could this explain why you left school, for a medical appointment, yesterday?"

"I don't understand, it's not possible!" She replied, not actually answering the question she was asked. "I haven't lost any clothes and I don't even know what Rohypnol is."

"Rohypnol is commonly known as a 'designer drug', or a 'date rape' drug, and has occasionally been used in nightclubs. Apparently it is almost tasteless, and tends to be slipped in to the alcoholic drinks of unsuspecting women. The drink sometimes takes on a cloudy appearance. The victim often feels drowsy, and incapacitated after ingesting the drug, which acts as a muscle relaxant. For us, the annoying part of any investigation is that all traces of Rohypnol generally disappear from the victim's body within about twenty-four hours, which is why you are both being questioned with such a high degree of urgency," explained CSI Stermont. "Do either of you recognise any of these symptoms?"

"Hell, you'd better tell them Lauren, just to be safe," said Emma.

"Tell them what?" Mrs Bale asked.

"This morning I discovered that I have some unexplained bruising, and I can't remember anything after we ate our meal last night," Lauren replied. "I must admit to you that Mr Michael did turn up, unexpectedly, last night when we were sheltering in a cave, but he certainly wasn't there this morning when we woke up. The cave is full of his stuff; he's probably been living there for quite a while."

"I don't like what I'm hearing," commented Ms Waldron. "Are you telling us that you both arranged false alibis to be with Mr Michael last night? I feel sick with shame! How could you do this? Anything could have happened to you both. God only knows what this will do to your good reputation. Both girls clasped hands, and lowered their heads, without answering. Let's hope, for Mr Michael's sake, that the police find him before I do!"

"No, no, no, it's nothing like that! It just happened by accident. We didn't even know he was supposed to be missing!" Lauren replied, angrily. A long silent pause followed, as CSI Stermont recommenced writing in her note pad.

"Mrs Bale, Ms Waldron, do we have your permission to take both girls for medical examinations and blood screening, including toxicological analysis?" asked CSI Stermont. "This will enable us to verify whether, or not, they have recently been subjected to any form of inappropriate assault." Both women nodded, too shocked to comment. "We will obviously need to confirm your daughters' versions of events with forensic evidence taken from the scene, and to formally interview and fingerprint both girls in due course, before determining what action, if any, should be taken."

CSI Stermont accompanied Emma and Joanna Waldron as they left the room, enabling DC Turnbull to raise an extra issue with Lauren. "Miss Bale, Mr Clarke informs me that earlier today, you handed him a school blouse belonging to another missing person, Angela Stoker. Can you explain how this came to be in your possession?"

"Lauren, I suggest you don't answer any further questions at the moment," advised her concerned mother. She turned to face Lauren, and reassuringly held her hand. "You're likely to set yourself up as a suspect, if you're not careful! As you can imagine, this news has come as rather a huge shock. We'll need to talk this through when we get home. It's best if you remain silent until then. In the morning I'll ask a lawyer-friend from Chase-Brooke's to sit in with us during any further interviews, to protect your interests."

CHAPTER THREE

"Wake up, Alexia," said Steve, abruptly, as he parked the car outside of her apartment building on the outskirts of Longbarrow.

"What's the panic?" She replied, whilst attempting to open her eyes.

"There's somebody in your flat! I swear I just saw a silhouetted figure pass behind your living room curtain," said Steve.

"Just what I need right now – what with crabs eating body parts, a flying car and cave-dwelling kids. How much more excitement can a girl take?" Alexia replied, not taking his comments seriously. "It's been a long day, so don't mess me around just now, it's just not funny anymore!"

"Wouldn't you like me to check it out for you?" Steve asked, trying his best to appear concerned and supportive.

"Oh, if you insist – come in for a quick drink, but you can't stay long," she replied, "I need to check through my paperwork in readiness for an early start tomorrow morning. Fancy a trip to the beach as soon as the tide heads out? I'll need to get a team down to the cove to process the cave that those girls mentioned, as well as coordinating a finger-tip search around the location where that Mondeo was found."

"Have you checked the tide times?"

Alexia panicked as she realised the logistical error she had already made by arranging for six colleagues to meet her at 6am, before the commuter rush started. "I think we'll do the fingertip search at the cliff top first, so that we don't attract too much attention from bystanders, and then take the dinghy out to the cove, rather than clambering over wet rocks – shall we say about 8.30am to meet at the seafront?"

"That's fine with me," replied Steve.

"These recent events seem unusual to me – when was that teacher reported missing? I'm surprised Jamie didn't mention it to me when I last saw him."

"We had the first call late on Friday evening, after the school secretary phoned his home number to find out why he didn't turn up for work. His mother was staying at his house at the time, and said that he definitely headed off to the school, as normal, but didn't return home later that day. Apparently, it was her birthday, and he had booked to take her out for a meal. Our receptionist told her that a person has to be missing for twenty four hours before an official missing person report can be filed. We received another (anonymous) call about his disappearance early this morning, shortly before the car was recovered, which has raised my suspicions that there might be an element of foul play involved. That's why I requested for you to be assigned to this case, to work alongside me. What, with your good looks, and my brains, we'll crack it in no time, besides, I'll get to eat posher meals if your department is footing the bill!"

"Don't bank on it – I'm planning on having a detox week!" Alexia chuckled, whilst removing her door key from her jacket pocket, and casually entering her apartment.

"What a cool cat! Not even a sign of nerves when you walked in – very impressive!" Steve exclaimed. He located and flicked the light switch to illuminate the room and then quickly checked the room for signs of any unauthorised entry before allowing Alexia to enter.

"You must just have seen the silhouette of trees, backlit by the moonlight, if anything, coming from the opposite window. Anyway – my curtains are wide open during the day, therefore, I knew it would have been extremely unlikely for you to have seen anyone passing behind them."

"I'm sure you won't blame a guy for trying," he quipped, in awe of her quick-wittedness, and meticulous attention to detail. "There'll be a day when you'll be caught with your guard down and, you never know, you might appreciate me being there for you." Alexia smiled sweetly at his remarks, as she lit a candle in an essential oil burner on the hearth, and added few drops of patchouli oil. "I didn't know you were into all that hippy oil stuff," he remarked.

"You should feel honoured, rather than mocking it. Patchouli oil is used as a base ingredient in most of the really high quality, expensive perfumes. Anyway, this might help mask the dank smell of Jamie's dog. He brought it round last night after letting it swim in the in the sea."

"That's the second time you've mentioned Jamie. Are you playing me off against some other beau?" Steve asked, disappointedly.

Alexia sniggered. "He's my kid brother – didn't you know? Actually, to be more precise, he's my half brother. My mum re-married, when I left home to go to university, which was a few years after my grandad died, and Jamie was born a couple of years later. Grandad had a fatal heart attack when he intercepted a burglar whilst I was still at school, so I never got the chance to say goodbye. We got on really well; he even left this flat to me in his will. He's the main reason why I trained to be a scene of crime investigator – determined to nail all the bad guys! I hope that if he ever looks down on me, he'll be proud of what I've achieved." She pointed to the large, elegant mahogany wall display unit, which housed her collection of childhood sports trophies and an assortment of family memorabilia. "There's a photo of us both together, on the shelf if you want to take a look."

"Anyhow, where's that drink you dragged me here for?" Steve asked her.

"Be a star, and turn the kettle on, will you? I'll have a black coffee, please, though you can have a fruity tea, instead, if you wish," said Alexia, smirking. She knew he'd prefer a beer, or something stronger, but wasn't prepared to encourage him to drink and then drive home afterwards.

Steve had become a close friend to Alexia, since the Forensic Science Service (FSS) team relocated to labs and offices within the same building as the Lychford-Green Police Station at the beginning of the year. He had gradually learned to trust her judgement implicitly, despite the fact that he and his colleagues knew very little, if anything, about her past life, apart from being aware that she had transferred from the FSS research and development facility, after working on a beta-test version of a new DNA profiling technique, and that a long-term boyfriend had abandoned her, a few years ago, whilst they were holidaying in the Maldives.

This latest revelation about Alexia's family confirmed that Steve was, at last, starting to chip through her personal exclusion zone, and gaining the confidence of the lady whom he admired and respected more than anyone he had ever met. Despite their obvious attraction to each other, Alexia was not yet ready to let another man into her life; preferring to keep her social and professional lives separate. Sheer perseverance, and working long unsociable hours, had earned her a reputation as being a formidable investigator, with one of the highest prosecution success rates in the county.

"What's that you mentioned about a crab, eating body parts?" Steve asked. "Have I missed out on some obscure girlie joke, or something?"

"I thought maybe it was your sick sense of humour at first, when I saw the bucket on my desk and then the smell of rotting flesh hit me!" She winced at the memory of the event. "The stench was unbelievable."

"I still have no idea what you're whittering on about. What bucket?" Steve asked, obviously somewhat annoyed that he had been bypassed in the office gossip loop.

"How could you not know about this, since it's in your patch?" Alexia wasn't really expecting an answer. "The skipper of the 'King Arthur' trawler radioed the coastguard about his unusual catch as soon as he landed his lobster pots whilst still at sea yesterday morning. He noticed that a large crab of some sort was clenching the severed foot, just as he was about to tip his haul into a holding tank. Two of our local officers met the boat as it moored up in the afternoon, recovered the evidence and took photos. Meanwhile, a team of Royal Navy frogmen were dispatched to check the sea-bed for any other human remains, at the coordinates that the skipper provided to us, but unfortunately, they didn't find anything. Apparently, the coastguard will continue to monitor the beaches and coves along this stretch of coastline over the next few days to see what the tide washes ashore."

"What happened to the rest of the crabs and lobsters?" Steve asked.

"The guilty crab is in a tank of sea water, in the lab, blissfully unaware of the commotion it has caused. Luckily, it was the only one in that particular lobster pot. It will probably be handed to one of the SeaLife sanctuaries when this investigation is complete. The enormous size of the creature suggests that it could be a lot older than we are, and I'm sure the publicity surrounding its discovery will make it quite a tourist attraction. The other crabs were collected from more distant locations, and were therefore sent for processing as normal, after inspection. The small catch of fish, mainly mackerel, was released for sale, since they were deemed very unlikely to have been in contact with the same food source as the crustaceans."

"There'll be uproar when the local newspaper gets wind of this – there's bound to be a backlash! You know – suggestions of involuntary cannibalism, and the like."

"Maybe – we'll have to wait and see. I'm betting that the foot belongs to the missing girl, Angela Stoker. It certainly seems to belong to a female, owing to remnants of bright pink nail varnish on the toes," commented Alexia.

"How long till the tests come back?"

"It's normally about two weeks for non-urgent routine chemical analysis, since samples get sent to the government laboratories in Wales. We do this because we need to be able to call on staff that can appear as 'expert witnesses' when this case gets to court. Forensic scientists cannot be expected to be experts in all fields, however well qualified they are, and these types of samples are not my area of expertise. I have already escalated the analysis to a 'high priority' status, so we could receive some results in less than forty-eight hours if we're lucky, but that would depend on same-day courier delivery of the samples."

"That sounds reasonable enough," he replied.

Photographic evidence of Angela's bedroom reveals make-up items, so they'll need to run chromatographic analysis to check the chemical profiles of all pink-coloured nail varnish samples we can obtain from her family. The fact that the foot has been in sea water compromises much of the remaining evidence, owing to the huge variety of contaminating genetic material that is contained in the surrounding water. Our pathology team hopes to isolate sufficient bone and muscle tissue, rather than the external rotting layer, to help identify the owner. Mitochondrial DNA is our best tool I think,' she replied, knowing that Steve would be impressed, yet flummoxed, by any technical detail.

"You've lost me, kiddo! I thought there was only one sort of DNA," he replied, "you know, the sort we had to spent hours drawing at school, while the teacher sneaked off into the science prep room for a coffee break."

"There's nuclear DNA, from a cell's nucleus, and Mitochondrial DNA that we can isolate. The mitochondrial sort is more abundant, since there are between one hundred and a thousand mitochondria in each cell of the body, and they all contain the same information. The downside of this is that it is always maternally inherited, basically, meaning that it's passed from mother to child, with no link to the father. The positive side is that there should be more of this in the sample than from other organisms that have been in contact with the foot before it ended up in the bucket on my desk, so at least we'll be able to match it up to the body when we find it," she explained.

"I gather that you're expecting to find a dead body, rather than this being a severed foot from a living person, then?" He asked.

"Maybe," she replied.

"We'll need to be very careful when approaching the family with this news of the gruesome discovery – I'll gladly send an appropriately trained officer to do this, and offer them 'victims of crime' support, unless you've already sanctioned something. Can you imagine the heartbreak caused by informing a mother of a dead child, only to find that he or she is in fact alive, and has merely suffered an amputation?"

"There's nothing mere about an amputation, anyway, you're jumping the gun a bit, aren't you? Let the science do the talking when the results are back, shall we?" Alexia replied. "There's already some forensic evidence that maybe we can match to the Stoker missing person case, with a possible link to one of the girls that we talked to this afternoon. Microscopic analysis of a dark-brown hair extracted from Angela Stoker's school blouse reveals a damaged cuticle at the point where the root has pulled from the scalp. In a normal healthy person, this bulb section is intact, however, if a hair is removed from a person that is already dead, the bulbous root section can appear fractured, which is what we have found in this case. We are running further tests to compare the mitochondrial DNA from the hair shaft to samples that we have already taken from Angela's hair brush. If there is a match, then we can assume that it is highly probable that Angela has already died, but we need considerably more evidence to support this. DNA evidence on its own never stands up in court, particularly since it can so easily be transferred to the surface of an object by just touching it with your hands."

"I wish I'd never asked," Steve stated.

"I've brought paperwork home to look through tonight, so I'll have a better idea how to progress with this tomorrow."

"Fascinating, but rather morbid, don't you think? Most people settle down with a good book and a glass of wine or something in the evening. You always seem to keep working, as if you owe the world a favour. How do you manage to detach yourself emotionally from all of this, eh? It would destroy me."

Alexia just smiled, as their eyes met.

Steve rested his hand on her shoulder. "Promise me you won't work too hard tonight – we'll have more than enough to deal with tomorrow. See you at the café on the beachfront at eight-thirty then?"

She blushed slightly, whilst coyly nodding her response, before stepping backward slightly to avoid the embarrassment of the anticipated good-night embrace. Their hands brushed together briefly.

"I'll even buy you a filter-coffee, if you're on-time," chuckled Steve, as he raised his hand to wave goodbye, and headed towards the door.

"That's a date then," replied Alexia, quietly, when Steve was just out of ear-shot, "by far the best offer I've had all year!" She waited for the door to close, before kicking off her uncomfortable high-heeled shoes, throwing her expensive designer jacket onto the back of the well-worn sofa, and loosening her long, wavy, black hair from a plait. Away from the full-on attention of her colleagues, she finally felt comfortable enough to relax in front of the fire, with a glass of ice-cold Chilean white wine in her hand, reminiscing, as always, of happier times. Early career promotions, in what she perceived to be a traditionally male-dominated environment, had forced the six-foot, blue eyed, sallow-skinned, thirty-two year old to mask her naturally shy demeanour, in favour of an outwardly business-like appearance and the yuppie go-get attitude to life.

CHAPTER FOUR

"Amazing, Miss Stermont!" Steve exclaimed, as Alexia approached, wearing her blue forensics-issue dungarees, sturdy walking boots, and a high visibility jacket. "What a sight, first thing in the morning – you look like one of the members of 'Village People' dressed like that."

"Whatever takes your fancy, Steve! I'm sure you'll also look this glamorous when we head to the cave. It's a restricted area, so we'll also be wearing hard hats, as a precaution against rock fall," she replied. "Where's that coffee you promised me then? Is there chance of a bacon roll to go with it?"

"Breakfast is booked for eight-thirty, as agreed," he replied, whilst checking his watch, "you're a couple of minutes earlier than expected." He now knew Alexia well-enough to realise that, unless there were specific breaks allocated throughout the working day, she would probably not stop to eat anything until she returned home. "Have you had any success so far this morning?"

"Yes, I think so. Whoever pushed the car over the

cliff had some knowledge of how to foil the forensics trail. We recovered footprints – not near to where the car would have been, but a considerable distance up the road instead, paced out as if the perpetrator stopped, then ran across the road, at which point the footprints cease. We're looking for a size eight shoe with a distinctive trainer-style tread. We'll run the image through our database of shoe profiles – it shouldn't take long once the image is scanned into the computer. It appears that he discarded a set of used latex gloves and plastic overshoe covers, which Nikki recovered from the bushes. She's taken these back to the lab now, for fingerprinting and DNA profiling, and will also perform shoe imprint analysis on the inner surfaces of the overshoe covers. I'm hoping for some preliminary results later today."

"Excellent! Presumably the gloves will have traces of sweat inside, as well?"

"Yes, I should think so. My hands certainly sweat when I wear them, which makes them quite tricky to get off again afterwards. In any case, there is bound to be some excreted oil and a few skin cells we can test – we don't require large samples anymore. The 'DNAboost' software that we're trialing should help separate DNA jumbles from the most miniscule amounts of sampled material. Take for example, if the culprit has recently shaken hands with someone, or perhaps has stroked a cat, there's a good chance we'll soon know about it," Alexia explained. "This latest find might suggest why we didn't detect palm print evidence on the rear or sides of the car, yesterday, when we processed it. The exterior paintwork of the red Ford Mondeo had obviously been washed and polished recently, so most of the fingerprints we've dusted and lifted were mainly isolated to the driver's door and boot lock area. So far, there have been no hits to match these on the National DNA Database, so we're checking against those held at local police stations. If our databases fail to turn up a positive match, then I have an idea on how we might overcome this hurdle for any suspects associated with the Allen Mead School."

"Brill! I just hope it's legal, since we may have to present it in court. Anyway, hold up a little, have your bacon butty before it gets too cold, then tell me more about it, if you wish," said Steve.

"Ben found several traces of blood residue on the underside of the car's front nearside bumper yesterday. We're not sure what source this came from, or indeed, when it occurred. Since most people don't tend to wash or polish underneath a car, it's one of the places we tend to check very carefully for evidence of the driver's activities. As a precaution, I checked Mr Michael's car insurance details last night – there are no reported accidents logged on his record," she added, before Steve gesticulated for her to stop talking, and to finish her breakfast.

"Mrs Bale is due at the station with her daughter, later today, I believe. Are there any blood results back yet?"

"Not as far as I know. Lyndsay hopes to be able to phone the results through sometime this morning, when she's had time to check the chromatograms from the overnight toxicology scan. Some good news though – last night the medical examiner gave the girls an all-clear on any physical evidence of sexual abuse, which is a huge relief."

"That will make my job a lot easier – rape cases are notoriously difficult to get to court, as well you know. Were they fingerprinted?" Steve asked.

"Not yet – that's your department's jurisdiction at the moment, until we secure forensic evidence that we need to check them against," she replied.

"What ideas do you have for overriding the normal fingerprint analysis route then? You'd better let me have the details before I end up having to cover-up any indiscretions for you."

"Don't worry. I've got a reputation to keep. I thought we could apply to might make use of the thumbprint recognition library access system at the school. It stores an algorithm rather than an image of the thumbprint itself, though I'm not sure if it will identify a person from a photocopy or digital image of a thumb print. Perhaps we could mock-up a synthetic prosthetic thumb from any data we obtain, if a three-dimensional image is required for the library access system to work. It's a long-shot, I know, but I'm trying to think ahead, keeping all options open. I thought maybe it could be useful in Angela Stoker's case, mainly to track her movements during the last couple of weeks. I suppose it's best to wait for a while and see what the cave reveals first shall we?"

"You're quite right – we'll follow standard procedures for now, if you don't mind. Shall we get some work done then?"

"Let's pretty you up a little then!" Alexia suggested, disappointed at the less than enthusiastic response to her novel idea. "Liam is waiting outside now – he's got spare overalls, a high visibility vest, and also a safety helmet for you."

"Oh, joy! I hope they fit better than yours!" Steve joked, bemused at the five centimetre gap between the bottom of Alexia's trousers and her hiking boots.

"Oh, I get it now – you're obviously just jealous!" She responded, with mocked indignity. "We're heading over to the rocks, to check where Emma Waldron said she left her bag. Whilst we're doing that, Liam and Adam will take the dingy round the cove, since the tide's still high. They will rig up a generator for the lighting, which will allow all areas of the cave to be searched." She reached into her pocket, removing a water-proofed container, containing a testing kit, and a digital camera, which she removed, then hung around her neck. "Here, Steve – you'll need gloves when we get there."

"Yes, I realise that, but thanks anyway. It's great to be out on the front line again, for a change, though I'm really surprised at how many call-ins we've had during the last few days."

"That's the reason why we've been authorised to use all available personnel for this search today – we need to be seen to act quickly on this, before the media and the chief hound us for it. Circumstances suggest that there's a significant link between Mr Michael being reported missing and the two girls spending a night away from home, as well as between the Bale family and Miss

Stoker's disappearance," Alexia replied, as she casually took photos of the beach and cliff setting, using Steve as a height marker.

"I quite agree. It's quite a tangled-web of events, isn't it?"

"The girls would have seen these large signs warning them to keep off the rocks, so what must have gone through their tiny minds to chance coming here?"

"You know what kids are like – they've got an inbuilt mechanism to challenge everything, even more so when they become teenagers. They seem to believe they're invincible – that no matter what they do, they'll never come to any harm. All part of growing up I suppose. I know that I was just the same. Didn't you ever do anything reckless as a kid?"

"Yes, I suppose so, but nothing really dangerous. One thing I remember doing regularly is that I used to wait at the bottom of shop escalators, until they were crammed full with people, then hit the stop button – giggling as everyone fell over. I never tired of it. How about the young Steve Turnbull – are there any blots on your character?"

"I used to enjoy playing practical jokes, just like everyone else. Putting twigs in my brother's bed, and waiting for him to scream, thinking it was a spider, was one of my favourites, oh, and putting clingfilm over the school toilets was another. I recall that I got a few detentions after several kids managed to wee all over the floor, but it was worth it just to see the look on their faces as they came back to class with wet clothes. Wicked, eh?"

He chuckled to himself as the memories of youthful exploits and adventures flooded back to him.

Alexia caught Steve's gaze. She tried to stifle her giggles at the thought of her friend ever being a naughty school boy. "Okay, okay, let's move, shall we?" She said, in an attempt to change the conversation. "Look over there. That's possibly where Emma slipped, when she hurt her ankle. The edge of the boulder has white scuff marks, with what appears to be blood spatter lower down," Alexia stated, as she moved forward to take close-up photo, with a ruler for scale comparison, and a numbered marker beside it. "It looks like capillary bleed, judging from the spatter pattern; it's not characteristic of a deep wound. Can you swab it please, Steve, whilst I get the evidence tube marked up ready for the lab?"

"No problem," he replied, "there's quite a nice blood trail for once. You mark it all up, and I'll follow behind. I'd like a photo shot from above when you've done, please, so that I can get a clearer view of the whole scene of action."

"Yes, sure Steve, I'm on to it!" She was slightly surprised that Steve felt the need to remind her how to do her job properly. Her reputation for attention to detail when collecting evidence from crime scenes was well-renowned. "Over here for a minute, Steve. There's a superb fossil I'd like you to see – it's an ammonite, I think. It's coated with what appears to be iron pyrite. What a stunner! This must be the place where my step-dad collected the large fossil that I use as a paperweight at work."

"Don't get side tracked, kiddo! Anyway, I didn't think you were supposed to remove that sort of thing from its natural setting – it's like destroying historical records."

"Apparently, beachcombing is okay, but fossil hunters are encouraged not to tap away at the rock face with their hammers. I am informed that just sifting through the course sand at the base of this cliff will allow most people to go home with some type of fossil. The ones close to the pyrite seam appear to be the best preserved, and most sought-after."

"Yes, I suppose that's logical. It's probably why the council have restricted the public access to this area, to stop ill-equipped silly devils climbing on the rock face," replied Steve.

"Anyone who accessed those girls' school bags will undoubtedly have come into contact with the iron pyrite dust, which gradually oxidises to form rust when exposed in this environment. That's why we can see those reddish-brown stains on the limestone rock. Believe it or not, this could be a really good find for us, Steve. Hand me a plastic specimen tube will you? I'll take a control sample of this pyrite, for reference purposes."

"Sure, but who'd have thought an ammonite could help solve a crime millions of years after it died? This says a lot for modern policing methods!" He joked. "Just wait till the media catches wind of this – there'll be a loads of fishy headlines in the papers."

"Oh, do be serious, Steve! We've got a job to do. I'll need to request a few extra analyses now on any fingerprints recovered from Emma's lunch box, and also on Lauren's school blouse. We'll need to screen for iron sulfide, iron oxide, and calcium carbonate."

"You know I'm not a chemist, so will you tell me what you mean?"

"Sorry," she replied, "they're commonly known as iron pyrite, rust, and limestone."

"You might want to bag this, Alexia."

"What have you found?"

"Something you'll really thank me for; dog excrement!" He chuckled, "it smells really ripe, so it's probably quite recent."

"Lucky me! We'll need a manila envelope first, to reduce any likelihood of fungal growth, then an outer-bagging of polythene. As a special treat, when we've got it bagged and tagged, and the seals have been signed, I'll let you carry your discovery over to the evidence box in the cave," she replied.

The cave was awash with light, rather like a high-calibre themed night-club; attracting much attention from the sightseeing yachting enthusiasts that had gathered offshore. A temporary bridge structure could be seen spanning the cave mouth and the surrounding rocks, as well as a floating jetty, thus allowing the forensics team to carry equipment to and from the site, irrespective of the tide status.

"Hi there, Steve!" Liam shouted, from the back of the cave. "We are just about to go with 'lights out', so come on in, making sure that you're on a sure footing – we don't need any accidents to spoil the scene," he warned, before initiating an ultraviolet scan of the cave's contents.

"What are you checking for?" Steve asked.

"Anything and everything, I suppose. Non-visible body fluids and other materials that fluoresce can be detected by this method," he replied.

"This place smells like a mixture of rotting seaweed and a toilet. Not somewhere I'd choose to live or camp out for any period of time," Steve commented.

"It could be worse, believe me!" Adam responded. His head could just be seen emerging from behind a large boulder, to the side of the cave. "Caves, like these, often fill with litter and dead sea-birds, washed in on the tide, which ultimately fester as they decompose. Luckily, for our sakes, this place is relatively dry, and clear of debris at present, though I suspect somebody has made great efforts to clean up here."

"What are you holding there, Steve? Your sandwiches?" Liam enquired.

Steve looked down to his evidence bag, parts of which were now glowing brightly in the beam of ultraviolet light. "I wish!! This is fresh dog poo from the rocks, near to where one of the girl's bags was left," he replied. "Where is the evidence box?" Liam gestured him towards a large plastic crate near to where he was standing.

"Walk on the white plastic sheet please – everything else still needs to be processed." The sheet itself was glowing brightly in the fluorescent light.

"And to think that it was *you* who complained of the smell in here!" Liam laughed. "Judging from the fluorescence, that belonged to a cat, not a dog, but non-the-less, we'll process it just the same. It's obviously soggy enough to have penetrated the manila inner envelope. He chuckled quietly to himself. "Did Alexia set you up for that one?"

"Hmm, I very much doubt it, somehow. She's not like that, is she? Anyway, have you found anything useful here so far?" Steve asked, trying to change the subject.

"Quite a few footprints, flipper imprints, sweet wrappers, hairs, and clothing fibres that might be useful to us, as well as locational evidence of an object having been dragged along the floor. There are also a few scorch marks in the grits; presumably from some sort of fire. It may have been an area set-aside for cooking – we'll soon find out," replied Adam. "It's been quite a productive couple of hours. It usually takes a lot longer than this to process a scene. We're planning to dust-up for fingerprints next, when we go 'lights-on' again in a minute or two. Stay where you are until then, please."

"Don't worry guys," shouted Alexia, as she climbed into the cave mouth, "I'll take responsibility for looking after him."

"Glad you could join us – what kept you?" Steve asked.

"I was checking out a rock pool – seems that

someone might have handled one of the resident sea-slugs before placing it back in the pool. There is a little of the purple, ink-like substance that it secreted on the nearby rock, so we must assume that whoever touched it will have some on his or her clothing as well. The down-side is that it can eventually be washed off, with a little effort." She turned towards her friend, and spoke quietly. "Steve, I'd like to talk to you about this, later, when we're alone, if you don't mind."

"Sounds intriguing, maybe over a coffee at the beach café again, after we've finished here?"

"Good idea – we'll be able to grab a quick lunch as well, before I head back to write-up my report based on my notes and sketches," she replied.

"We're done here, so let's have lights on again, please," shouted Liam.

"Hi, Alexia," said Adam, "I think we might just have made a significant break-through here. If I recall correctly, Mrs Stoker's interview transcript stated that the only jewellery her daughter was wearing to school, on the morning she disappeared, was a brand new Accurist watch which had a blue leather strap. I have just recovered a ladies' watch which closely matches that description. Hopefully, latent fingerprint analysis, back at the lab, will reveal something to link the watch with the owner."

"Where was it?" Alexia enquired.

"It was lodged in a crevice, near to the west-wall of the cave. The UV light illuminated the face of the watch, which is probably coated with a luminescent paint.

Scrape marks close to the crevice, show that someone has obviously tried, unsuccessfully, to retrieve it with a sharp object. I've initiated taking imprints of the area already."

"That's great news. Have you been able to lift any fingerprints yet?" She asked.

"No, we're about to start dusting all surfaces now. Are you offering to help us? We need to wrap this up quite quickly, as we're on quite a tight schedule today."

"Sure, I'll be glad to help out," she answered, whilst delving into her shoulder bag. "Pass me a spare brush, tape, marker pen and a tub of aluminum powder, will you?"

"Where is yours then, boss? Isn't there any in your kit?" Adam asked.

"I could have sworn there was. I checked everything a couple of days ago, as soon as we received this case call, and haven't had the need to use anything other than specimen bags since then."

"Has anyone had access to your kit?" He asked.

"Not that I'm aware of – I usually keep it stored at home." She looked over at her probationary colleague. "Hey, Lorne, did you manage to retrieve anything from the Post Office phone box?"

"Nothing of any real consequence, Miss Stermont, just few white cotton fibres from the handset, but no useable fingerprints at all. There were loads of partial prints on the windows and framework, as you'd expect from a well-used public phone, though the door handle and phone equipment itself appears to have been chemically wiped clean."

"That's a real shame. What about CCTV footage?"

"We drew a blank with that one as well, I'm afraid. There doesn't appear to be one in that location," replied the new recruit.

"There's not much else we can do with that, at the moment, apart from interviewing members of the public who may have seen something. Steve, this is your call – will you be handling it?"

"Perhaps, if you can convince me that it's relevant to this case, and not simply a fanciful whim based on Miss Waldron's interpretation of events. The other girl hasn't mentioned seeing anyone resembling Mr Michael being in that location. I really don't have the manpower and resources to allow me to embark on a wild goose chase. You'll need to get your guy, Lorne, to check details with the phone company to see if a call was actually made within the timeframe we're interested in, and then I'll decide whether or not to make my men available to interview the local shoppers and retailers."

"That's fair enough! Meanwhile, let's grab that coffee and something to eat," commented Alexia, as she bade goodbye to her team for the afternoon.

"What's so important that you need to speak to me privately then?" Steve asked, as he pushed down the plunger in the four-cup capacity cafetière. "You're not usually that secretive."

"I'm slightly worried that my brother, Jamie, could somehow be embroiled in this latest missing person case."

Steve reached across the wooden table, and reassuringly rested his hand on hers. "Take your time, and talk me through what's bothering you and we'll find a solution."

"There might be circumstantial evidence that links him to the cave vicinity on the night that the two girls claim to have spent with Mr Michael, which he hasn't mentioned to me. It's odd, but I thought I vaguely recognised Lauren Bale when we chatted to her yesterday – she could possibly be a friend of his. They're about the same age, and do attend the same school. Something doesn't feel right."

"What has aroused your suspicions?" Steve asked. "You can't doubt the lad just because he's a twelve year old, besides, he already told you he took the dog for a swim in the sea that evening, didn't he?"

"Sure. It's just that I can't allow my judgement to be compromised. On Monday evening he arrived with a purple stained shirt, very similar to the sea-slug secretion that I came across today. I can't be involved in any criminal investigation that involves members of my own family, as you well know, so do me a favour, and talk to him about this will you?"

"Leave it with me, Alexia. I'll arrange to call in on him after I've finished the interview with the Bales, sometime later this evening."

"Thanks, Steve, you're a star!" Alexia leant forward and kissed her blonde-haired friend on his stubbly cheek, causing him to blush profusely. She smiled at the unexpected reaction to her kiss, noting his endearing vulnerability. "Let's have a look at the menu then, shall we? I owe you big time for this, so lunch is on me today – I'll let you treat yourself to a luxury sandwich!"

"Last of the big spenders, eh?" He replied, sarcastically, whilst trying to avoid catching her gaze.

"You know me – all heart!" She chuckled. "Hey – I'm sorry!"

"Don't be," he replied, "you caught me off-guard – that's all." There were a few minutes of awkward silence. "Do you have any results from Lyndsay yet?"

"Fortunately, yes. The toxicology results indicate that neither of the young girls had detectable amounts of Rohypnol in their blood at the time of analysis, however, they both had appreciable amounts of alcohol present, which explains why they felt so groggy."

"What sort of levels are we talking about?" Steve asked. "It will be useful information to discuss at the interview this afternoon."

"Emma's was the highest result, with just over thirty milligrams per one hundred millilitres of blood, whereas Lauren had twenty-two milligrams per one hundred millilitres of blood. Considering that their levels would have dropped by about fifteen milligrams per one hundred millilitres of blood per hour since the time of consumption, we can assume they were almost certainly drunk and totally incapacitated at some stage during the previous evening."

"That's almost unbelievable – what were they trying to prove to themselves? That's enough alcohol to induce a coma, or alcohol poisoning in even the fittest of adults.

In my case, more than two beers, and I'm hopelessly wasted! I suppose those kids are luckier than they'll ever realise."

"True – in view of this, I consider we need to step up the search for Mr Michael as a matter of urgency. You never know, he may even be a victim of circumstance himself," said Alexia.

CHAPTER FIVE

"Lauren, will you please stop chewing your nails, and sit still for a while," said Elizabeth Bale, as they waited in the lobby at the police station. "They can't interview you until our lawyer gets here, so please be patient, and try not to work yourself up into a frenzy."

"What if they ask me lots of really personal questions, and stuff about the Stoker witch's disappearance? Do I have to answer everything?" She asked.

"If you feel uncomfortable with the type of question being asked, anything at all, just let Mr Standish know, and then follow his guidance. Technically, we're here co-operating voluntarily, so unless they have good reason to arrest you, I don't think they can demand any answers," replied Mrs Bale.

"It still doesn't help us very much, does it? The Stokers have been spreading nasty rumours about me and Robyn for months – ever since we called the council people in, and then had the noise abatement order issued against them. Everyone knows why I'm glad the silly witch is missing. I haven't made a secret of it."

"Never the less, Lauren, just be careful what you say to the police!" She replied, as she reassuringly patted her daughter's shoulder.

"Don't worry, mum, I'm not stupid!" Lauren exclaimed. "I really can be trusted to say the right thing, you know. You don't have to treat me like a child any more."

"You say that, Lauren, but the last couple of days have painted a very different picture of you; not that of the responsible person I thought you were. I hope you prove me wrong. I'm also still baffled about how you came to be wearing Angela's blouse the other day. I hope and pray that there's a clear explanation after the forensics people have tested it," replied her anxious mother.

"What are you saying? You don't trust me, do you?"

"I really don't know what to believe of you. Until I was called to the school yesterday, I thought I could trust you implicitly; however, it now transpires that you have been truanting from school, forging my signature, and have spent the night with a male teacher! It's been difficult enough bringing you two girls up on my own, since your dad died, and this is how you repay me. As always, you have my love and full support, but not my confidence at the moment."

"You spent hours grilling me about it last night, and telling me how lucky I am not to have been seriously hurt. I know it was all a huge mistake, and I've said sorry.

What more can I do to convince you?" She turned to face her mother, hoping for an answer, but it never came. "I have no idea where Angela's clothes came from, unless I accidentally picked up the wrong stuff at school, as I've already said," Lauren replied. She crossed her arms, turned away from her mother, and stared at the wall, huffing loudly in the process.

A few minutes later, the door swung open, and a tall well-dressed gentleman, carrying an expensive looking briefcase, entered the lobby area, his footsteps echoing loudly, as the shiny leather of his shoes made contact with the ceramic floor tiles. Mrs Bale stood and extended her hand to him as he approached. "Hello Elizabeth, it's so good to see you again," he said, "and this lovely young lady is your daughter, Lauren, I presume? Hi, I'm Dean Standish. I'll be representing you for as long as we need to clear up this unfortunate mess."

Lauren swivelled on her seat to face him, and nervously shook his hand. "Thank you. Have you any idea what's going to happen to me now? I'm completely innocent; I'm not involved in whatever they say I've done," Lauren remarked, rushing her words as if her life depended on it.

"There's nothing for you to worry about at the moment, Lauren. I have already spoken with DC Turnbull; there are a few questions he needs to ask you relating to Mr Michael and Miss Stoker, and then you'll be asked to sign a statement. Please do not answer any questions until you have conferred with me, and only provide relevant factual information, not hearsay or gossip. I expect that you will be fingerprinted first, for elimination purposes, and then a skin cell swab, called a buccal swab, will be taken from the inside lining of your cheek. It will be used for DNA comparison purposes, since you have already voluntarily given your consent. Assuming that you are not charged with any offence, this biometric information and your details will be destroyed when the case is complete," he responded.

Elizabeth and Lauren looked at each other; they were confused. "Mr Standish, I'm not sure what you mean by biometrics," said Lauren.

"Biometrics is simply a term used to describe the measurements taken from many types of biological information," he replied. "On a separate issue, I have been asked to inform you that our appointment has been delayed until about six o'clock – so we'll have time for a cuppa and to bring me up to date on recent events. Apparently the delay is to allow officers time to assess new information in the case that has surfaced this afternoon – quite literally, I gather."

"What type of new information?" Elizabeth asked him.

"I am not absolutely sure. I overheard some talk in the main office of a body being recovered off-shore by police divers. We'll just have to wait and see if this is linked to the case you're involved in. Either way, I suspect that this could be quite a long evening, so try not to get too worked up about it at the moment. Would you like me to organise drinks, before we find a vacant room for our discussions?"

"Thanks Dean, that's very thoughtful of you. We'll both have fresh orange juice, if it's available, please – nothing fizzy," replied Elizabeth.

"Have you told Robyn why I'm here yet?" Lauren asked her mum, as soon as Mr Standish left the room.

"Yes, to some extent, love. Gossip travels fast in your school, and I'm not going to lie to her," she replied.

"What do you mean? Who's been blabbing about me?"

"Obviously, Robyn is aware that you and Emma are in some sort of trouble, and are being interviewed by the police, mainly because of your truancy and whereabouts during Monday afternoon and evening. Naturally, she's concerned for you."

"Has she told you about who she saw on the beach on Monday evening, when she was there with Brett?" Lauren asked.

"She mentioned to me that she saw a man tussling and arguing with your friend, Jamie. The man ran off when Brett ran to intervene. Apparently, Jamie's dog was barking furiously, which is why it attracted their attention," replied Mrs Bale.

"Good for Sooty! It's not like her to cause a commotion – she's such an old, placid dog, so she must have sensed that Jamie was in danger."

"Yes, I think so. Robyn thought the man resembled photos that she has seen of Emma's dad, Mr Waldron, but couldn't be absolutely sure, since it was quite dark, and he was silhouetted," replied Mrs Bale. "I've already informed DC Turnbull, by phone, of this incident, just in case it has any relevance to what happened to you both during Monday evening."

"That's really not good news. Do Emma and Mrs Waldron know about this yet?"

"I'm not sure, love. DC Turnbull said he would arrange for someone to follow up all leads, however, he stressed that he couldn't discuss it any further with me. It all seems quite mysterious."

"You do know about Mr Waldron's background, don't you?" Lauren asked.

"Know what? Emma's parents divorced when she was very young, didn't they?"

"Yes, that's true to some extent. What you might not be aware of is that Mr Waldron is supposed to be serving a long term in prison for attempted murder, and several charges of assault. I've no idea when he's due for release. Emma and Mrs Waldron moved here, from Bristol, a few years ago, so that he wouldn't be able to find them," explained Lauren.

CHAPTER SIX

Alexia lit three vanilla-fragranced candles and opened the bathroom window slightly, before gracefully immersing herself in the steaming bubble-brimmed bath. She closed her eyes, and imagined the stresses of her busy day gently ebbing away to the feint sound of each wave crashing onto the beach, and receding away again far into the distance. Intermittent melodies from a songthrush perched high in the cherry tree outside added to the tranquillity – she felt calm and relaxed. She briefly slipped her head under the water, and swished vigorously from side to side to remove residual wind-blown sand and salt from her hair, before stepping out of the bath and wrapping herself in a towelling dressing gown. The phone was ringing.

"Hi Alexia, it's me, Steve. I hope I'm not disturbing you. I need to speak to you about Jamie."

"Hi! Is this about your meeting this evening? Did it go well?" Alexia asked.

"That's the problem. It couldn't take place."

"Why, what's happened?"

"I called in at his house at seven o'clock, after my interview with the Bales, but your mum said Jamie hadn't arrived home from school. It transpires that he was being followed by a man he confronted on the beach earlier in the week. In his panic, he hid behind a bush and then hopped on a bus as it pulled away from a bus-stop. He came directly here to the station instead, and is with me now. He is quite distressed, and is demanding to speak with you before he gets taken home. It's been a twelve hour day for me today, so I'm keen to go home as well," Steve replied.

"Okay Steve, I'll be there as quick as I can – just as soon as I'm dressed, and can get hold of a taxi."

"Can I presume you've got company tonight then?" Steve asked.

"No, no, certainly not, nothing like that – I've just had a bath!" She replied, indignantly.

"Don't bother with the taxi – make yourself presentable, and I'll send a car over for you. Your mum and step-dad are on their way here as well, so it will be like a family get-together for you all."

"Not much of a celebration, though I'm relieved that Jamie is okay."

"Don't you think it's about time you got your motor fixed, kiddo, rather than relying on me and taxis?"

"It's at the garage. Apparently, I should have it back by the end of the week. They say the hold-up is something to do with bent piston rods, and a typical woman driver!"

"Hmm – flash your badge at whoever said that to you, when you collect your vehicle – he'll think twice about being rude to you again. Maybe you'll remember to top the engine up with lubricant in the future, to keep it running properly."

As soon as Jamie caught sight of Alexia, he leapt to his feet, and threw his arms around her. His thick black hair clung to his reddened tear-stained face. She leant forward slightly to kiss him on the forehead, whilst reassuringly stroking his hair back into place with one hand, and holding him close to her with the other. At twelve years old, Jamie was taller than most boys in his class; now just tall enough to rest his head on his sister's shoulder, hiding his tears from onlookers. Alexia could feel his body trembling beneath his tattered school uniform, as he sobbed uncontrollably. She caught Steve's gaze, and subtly gestured for him to join her in an adjacent room. She shut the door, after asking Steve to bring another chair for himself, and moved her own chair next to her brother's so that she could reach and put her arm around his shoulder.

"Sorry, Lexi, I didn't know what else I could do," he sobbed. "I panicked, and didn't want him to find out where I lived, so I came here instead."

"Hey, I'm just glad you're safe!" Alexia replied. "You did the right thing." She fumbled in her handbag for a clean handkerchief, and offered it to Jamie, who preferred to wipe his eyes on his muddy sleeve. "Here, use this to blow your nose, and pretty yourself up a bit before DC Turnbull returns."

"I think it's the same guy that tried to grab hold of me at the beach the other day. I ran to your house afterwards, and think he might have been following me then, as well."

"Why didn't you tell me at the time?" She asked.

"I was too ashamed about the fight," he replied.

"Have you told mum and Mark about what happened?"

"No, I haven't, not yet anyway. I should have been at home that night, not at the beach with two girls. I was too embarrassed to admit it to them, I suppose. They told me they trusted me in the house on my own – now what will they think?" He replied. "I'll be grounded for sure!"

"Don't worry about that. The main thing is to keep you safe. Were you hurt at all?"

Jamie was about to answer, when the door opened, and Steve entered, balancing a tray full of drinks on the seat of the spare chair that he was carrying. "Have I missed anything important, Alexia?" He asked. "Your parents are here, Jamie. They're in the lobby, waiting for you."

"I think we'll be here a while," Alexia replied. "Could you try to occupy them, with a coffee or something, and then hurry back, please Steve? You'll need to log the description of the guy who's been stalking Jamie before we let him go home."

"No problem, leave it to me," he replied.

"Thanks, Lexi. I don't know what to say to them yet. I'm really confused. There's something else you need to know – I dropped my key-ring the other night when I ran home from your house, and it had your spare door key on it. I was too scared to stop and search for them. If the man followed me, he might have picked them up, and will already know where you live if he was watching me. I think he's dangerous."

Steve re-entered the room, carrying a lap-top computer, and sat opposite to Alexia and her brother. "Jamie, this is all a bit of a mess, isn't it? Can I deduce that you arranged to meet your school friends, Emma Waldron and Lauren Bale, on the night that you first met the man who has been stalking you?"

"Yes, that's right, but they weren't there, so I played with my dog, Sooty, for a while on the beach, until it started to get dark. I was about to head home, when Sooty ran towards a man who was climbing over the rockslide area – you know – that dangerous part around the cove where the caves are. He was looking through a girl's rucksack: it looked quite like Lauren's, so I went a bit closer, to find out what was going on. That's when he swore at Sooty, and threw something which hit her on the side of the face. Luckily, it just missed her eye. I ran over to where he was, and kicked him hard, grabbed hold of Sooty and ran back down the beach. He soon caught up with me, though thankfully my friends, Robyn and Brett, were there, and chased him off."

"That ties-up with what Mrs Bale told me this afternoon. Tell me – have you seen the man before?"

"No, I don't think so. I wouldn't forget his face though – he looked mean, really mean," Jamie replied. "He was unshaven, and smelt of bad body odour, like a tramp, you know, one of those people who never washes or changes their clothes."

Alexia leaned over to Jamie, and placed her arm around his shoulder again, whilst Steve typed on his computer. He arranged a series of images of known paedophiles and local prisoners on the screen, before turning it to face Jamie and Alexia. Before Steve had chance to ask a question, Jamie shouted that he recognised one of the men from the photos. "It's none of these men, but I recognise the guy with the curly blond hair and green eyes; he regularly hangs around the beach – I think he's one of those scuba divers. They've got some stuff up in one of the caves, I think."

"Hmm – that's quite useful to know," replied Steve. "How recently did you last see him?"

"I think it was last weekend, sometime, but I'm not sure. He hangs around with one of my teachers, and often says hello when I'm out fossil hunting and rock collecting with my dad."

Steve glanced at Alexia, signalling for her to cut the off-record conversation. "Would you be able to return here tomorrow morning, to give us a statement of events and write a full description of the man who confronted you on the beach, Jamie? This will allow one of my officers to generate a photo-fit image of him. It will take about an hour, so you'll miss a couple of lessons of school if you're lucky. You'll need to ask for PC Dingle when you arrive here; he'll help you to produce a good likeness of the suspect, using a computer graphics program. Meanwhile, I will be suggesting to your parents that they deliver and collect you from school, until we have located and interviewed the man in question."

Jamie nodded his response, and held his sister's arm as she escorted him to his parents.

"Are there any more family members you'd like me to meet?" Steve asked, sarcastically. "If there are no more re-unions or introductions on the agenda for tonight, I'll drive you home. We have another full day planned for tomorrow – I hope you're not squeamish!"

"What do you know that I don't?" Alexia replied.

"We've recovered a female body. It might be the young girl we're looking for. A speedboat hit it in the bay, whilst we were processing the cave earlier. Apparently it damaged the boat's propeller. We'll find out more details in the morning, when there are some preliminary pathology results."

"Shall we meet at eight-thirty again, at the café? It's my turn to buy breakfast. I owe you one, for helping my Jamie tonight."

"No worries – it's all part of the service. I suggest we start the day closer to nine o'clock, because unlike you, I need my beauty sleep. I'll pick you up, if you wish."

"That'll be great," replied Alexia. "It's been a hectic week so far. I think we've both earned a lie-in!"

"Don't be in a hurry to rush off. Let me walk you to your door, to check that everything's secure, and then I'll bid you goodnight."

"You're ever the gentleman – thank you," said Alexia as she fumbled through her handbag to find her door key.

CHAPTER SEVEN

Steve rang the doorbell several times before resorting to banging loudly on the door with his fist, and attempting to peer through the spy hole. Eventually the door opened fractionally, held ajar by the safety chain. "Alexia – it's me, Steve. Are you going to let me in?" There was no response, though he could hear somebody shuffling around in the room. "Don't mess me about, kiddo, I've got a job to do, three seconds, and I'll kick the door in!" He warned her. "Three, two, one…," and just as he prepared himself to forcibly open the door, it opened.

Alexia stood in front of him, still wearing her dressing gown, and giggling uncontrollably. "Hello darling …hic…"

"I don't believe it – you're drunk!"

"Mmm, subbose so," she giggled.

Steve guided her towards the sofa, steadying her with his arm, as she meandered across the room. A few minutes later, he emerged from the kitchen with a large mug of strong black coffee, to help her ward off the effects of a hangover. "Talk me through what's happening here, will you?"

She pointed at a bunch of keys next to the letterbox, and began to shake. "Shomewun put them froo the door jusd afder mindnide. I had a shmall drink tsoo help me shleep."

Steve tried not to snigger at his colleague's inability to pronounce her words properly, or at the slurping noises she made whilst trying to drink her coffee through her numb lips. "Are they *your* keys?"

"Yesh, looks like zem."

"You muppet! It's probably nothing more sinister than a considerate neighbour putting them through your letterbox – you probably left them in the lock on the other side of the door. I've managed to do that a few times, when I've been tired. Try not to worry about it. Meanwhile, let's get you sobered up a little, shall we?"

"Good idea, batman!" She replied, as she slipped off the edge of the sofa; knocking her coffee off the table, in the process. Steve glanced at her, rolled his eyes, and went in search of something to clean up the mess with.

"Have a cold shower and get yourself dressed, will you? Whilst you're doing that, I'll be outside. I'll borrow your keys for a short while, if you don't mind, so that I can let myself in again, after I've made an urgent phone call." Alexia looked up at him and nodded her approval. "I don't think you'll be showing up for work this morning, unless you make a really huge effort to get yourself sorted out. You'll never forgive yourself if you miss out on all the excitement, so snap to it, and try to get a move on please."

Alexia stood up and jokingly acknowledged Steve's commands by standing to attention and saluting him. He rolled his eyes again. This was a side of her he'd rather not have encountered.

"I dare say you'll be highly embarrassed by this later, kiddo. I hope you're in a better state when I return. I'll give you just over half an hour, and then I'll need to get to the station, whether you're with me or not."

The source of urgency was a message that Liam had just radioed through from the pathology lab, confirming that DNA results of analysis on the body and severed foot, recovered from the sea, were from the same person, and closely matched that from one of Angela Stoker's milk teeth that her mother, Mrs Sabrina Stoker had labelled, wrapped, and stored in her jewellery box for several years. The Infrared trace analysis of the nail polish sample taken from Angela's bedroom was also a perfect match to that scraped from the toe nails of the severed foot, found in the lobster pot on Monday morning. It was apparent that Steve now had the unenviable task of breaking the news of the find to the dead girl's parents, and arranging for them to make a formal identification of the badly decomposed body at the mortuary. Liam also advised Steve that Chief Inspector Gillian Lansing was preparing to deliver a carefully phrased press release, scheduled for a news conference at five o'clock, (which he would be required to participate at), so the body needed to be identified before mid-afternoon.

"Yes, this is my baby, detective, my beautiful darling,

Angie," wailed Mrs Stoker, trembling as Liam revealed the pallid face of the body, by partially removing the white sheet that had been covering the lifeless, naked body as it laid on the cold metal table. She leant down, and kissed her daughter gently on the forehead. "This doesn't seem real – just like a bad dream that I'll eventually wake from. It just isn't fair! Who could hurt my baby?" She mopped the tears from her face, and blew her nose, loudly. "How can this be real? Why Angie? What a sad, sad waste of such a young life – she had everything to live for." She looked over to her husband for reassurance, and support, but he remained motionless and silent, his head bowed low.

"I understand that this is a difficult moment for you both," said Steve, at which point Mr Stoker looked up and loudly interjected.

"Difficult? Is that all you've got to say, detective? Shame on you! We reported Angela missing over a week ago, and you told us to wait at least a day before you would look for her. Maybe, if you were more efficient, you would have checked the beach area, knowing how dangerous the rip-current can be. It seems that I'm the only person to have been out day and night looking for her! I haven't slept for days!" Liam and Steve glanced at each other.

"I can understand your frustration, sir. Please accept our sympathies for your loss. Be reassured that we have been fully employed in the search for your daughter. There is more to this case than a teenager simply misjudging the effects of the tide at the beach," commented Liam.

"What do you mean by that?" Mrs Stoker asked him.

"I mean that your daughter did not drown at sea, madam. There was an absence of sea-water in her lungs, which indicates that she was already dead before she entered the water. Close examination of the body revealed that she sustained a blunt trauma injury to her head, and what appears to be a further, unrelated impact injury to her upper leg and ribs. It is the head injury which would ultimately have caused her death," added Liam.

"We are awaiting results of forensic tests, and are following several lines of enquiry at present. We will obviously make it a priority to keep you fully informed, as we unravel the events leading to your daughter's death," said Steve, in an attempt to prevent Liam divulging any further details of the on-going investigation.

"When did she die?" Mr Stoker enquired.

"We're still trying to establish that information, sir, however, the soft tissue damage indicates that she may have been in the water several days before she was found, as this is the part that fish and crabs tend to nibble at first," replied Liam. There was no response to the comment. Liam and Steve signalled instructions to each other in their well-rehearsed sign language. After a brief pause, close to the body, the Stokers, held hands, turned, and attempted to leave the room.

On this cue, Steve moved forward, securing Mr Stoker's arm, and engaged him in conversation. He then manoeuvred him to a position which would produce a good closed circuit camera image of his face. So as not to raise any concern, Liam reassuringly rested his hand on Mrs Stoker's shoulder, and led her out of the room, chatting quietly.

"Mr Stoker, as we are now dealing with the suspicious death of your daughter, you'll appreciate that there are further questions that will need to be answered."

"Yes, I understand that there probably will be," he replied, sarcastically, before being formally arrested, and taken into custody.

"As a formality, both you and your wife are to be treated as suspects relating to the disappearance and manslaughter of your daughter, Angela, and will be detained to assist us with our enquires. A search warrant has been issued, which will allow our officers legal access to your home address. A search of the premises is underway as we speak." Mr Stoker remained silent and emotionless, as he was led away to an interview room.

"Thanks Liam. Did you encounter any problems with Mrs Stoker when you left, earlier?"

"Not until she was arrested by Dan. She looked more shocked than anything. She kept declaring her innocence, and stated that she needed her daughter's body to be blessed by a priest. She was also really anxious that there would be nobody to collect her son, Raheel, from school, so I informed her that someone from the Child Services Department would be allocated to look after him until further notice."

"Good stuff, Liam," Steve replied. "We need to get

this Stoker chap in an identity parade, pronto, since he appears to be quite a good match for the description that young master Jackson gave of the bloke that assaulted him on the beach on Monday evening. I'll lift a printout from the CCTV. image, and compare it with the photofit that was generated earlier. I've got a hunch that we've got a strong contender for the alleged attack in custody now. He, himself admits that he has been out day and night searching for his daughter."

"He strikes me as being an extremely odd character – too shifty for my liking," commented Liam. "What do you make of him? Would it be worth bringing in a psychological profiler to observe the interview sessions?"

"That's a sensible suggestion. Like you, I would have expected to see some display of emotion at the sight of a dead family member, especially when it involves a child. Even the most macho men crumble in that situation. We need to check Mr Stoker's alibis for the whole period of Angela's disappearance, as a matter of urgency."

"Yes, agreed – your department will be deluged with reporters after the press conference later, so I guess this will be our biggest profile case yet. A good job we have all the expertise under one roof now, eh?"

"Yes, agreed. It certainly has many advantages. Case turn-around times have improved considerably."

"I recall Alexia saying, at the last meeting, that one of Mrs Bale's daughters had reported a possible sighting of her friend's father, Mr Waldron, on the beach that night," said Liam.

"I checked that one out myself, earlier. It appears that

he's still banged up at Dartmoor Prison, and is not due for parole until next spring. A case of mistaken identity, I think, based on a few old photos that she had seen, however, I admit there is a significant facial resemblance between him and Mr Stoker. I think we need to get someone to check if there are any family ties linking Mr Stoker and Mr Waldron. It may well prove to be nothing, but would certainly help explain a few inconsistencies in this case."

"Leave it with me – I'll get our newbie, Lorne, on the task. He's out to impress the boss at the moment. Maybe he fancies his chances, or something."

"Talking of Alexia, has she arrived at work yet?"

"Yes, to some extent. She strolled in at about one o'clock, complaining that she wasn't feeling well, closed the window blinds, and promptly locked herself in her office. Nobody has heard a peep from her since then. It looks like she's just crawled out of bed, if you ask me. Is she unwell?"

"She had a late night here at the station, so I'm not surprised that she's in a bit of a state," said Steve, sniggering. "I'll try to shake her into action soon – she's probably asleep at her desk!"

"Thanks, we've got a few details relating to the post-mortem that need to be discussed, and then we can pass the report over to you guys."

"Significant finds, are they?"

"I'm sorry Steve, but I have to follow procedures, and pass this information up through my line management first, you know the rules," replied Liam, embarrassed at his lapse in confidentiality. "I don't have the authority to undermine my boss – the case could fall apart when it goes to court and, besides that, I could lose my job!"

"Is there enough evidence for a conviction?"

"Perhaps," Liam replied.

"To show willing, I'll go and rouse Alexia for you now, and let her know that I expect to discuss the post-mortem results with you both this afternoon, probably by phone, when she's fully functional. Meanwhile, I've received a lead that I need to follow up on, concerning Mr Michael. There's a chance I might not be back in time for the news conference, however, Alexia and Dan are fully briefed on the limited details that we will release to the press, just enough to keep them off our backs," replied Steve, as he exited from the room, slamming the door firmly behind him.

CHAPTER EIGHT

Steve was ushered through the long, echoing corridors, by the hoity, sombre-looking ward supervisor, towards the intensive care ward. They entered the last room on the left hand side, after being intercepted by a uniformed police officer, and required to produce valid security clearance identification for inspection. Once inside, they found a frail elderly lady waiting patiently on one of the brown plastic chairs next to the hospital bed, continually stroking the hand of the unresponsive patient. The erratic beeping of the wall-mounted heart monitor and the intermittent hiss of gas escaping from the ventilation mask, attached to noisy bellows which triggered every three seconds, indicated that the badly mutilated patient was desperately fighting for his life. His swollen, gashed face and bruised, bandaged, upper body rendered him virtually unrecognisable and unlovable to anyone other than his mother. Luke Michael was barely alive.

The coastguard had been alerted, by an anonymous caller, to sightings of an unidentified diver floating face-down off shore, several miles further up the coast. He had been shot through the back with a harpoon spear (which was still embedded in the diver's body when he was found), and left for dead. On-board paramedics arranged for him to be airlifted to King's College Hospital, London, on Tuesday morning, for emergency liver surgery, anticipating a very limited chance of survival for their patient.

It had taken three days to match the injured man's description to that of Mr Michael on the missing persons register. Clearly, somebody wanted him dead, perhaps considering him to be a threat of some sort. Local Metropolitan Police Officers, WPC Helen Lee, and PC John Jamieson, were in place already, offering round-the-clock security protection for the potential murder victim and his mother.

Chief Inspector Lansing had instructed that Mr Michael's discovery and survival should not be disclosed to the media, at least until the perpetrator had been apprehended. This was now a potential murder enquiry – the second case to be upgraded from missing person status in as many days.

Steve and his team now acknowledged that these events were extremely unlikely to be just a coincidence. He nurtured the idea that any secrets, infatuations, and fantasies penned into the murdered teenage girl's diary, linking her to the young male teacher, could ultimately be instrumental in revealing clues to her killer's motives. The difficulty would be separating fact from fiction from the locked-diary, which had been recovered from beneath

Angela's bed during the search of the Stoker's home. Two keys for the diary's lock were found – one hidden in Angela's underwear drawer, and the other in a tool box from the garage.

Steve signalled to the ward supervisor to leave the room shortly after she reprimanded him for using his mobile phone, in a clearly signed, mobile-prohibited area. "What's the news then Alexia?" He asked.

"It's quite odd really," she replied, "I have the results of the fingerprint analysis here. We lifted latent prints from the key in Angela's drawer, and there are two partials we can work with. One is from Angela's right thumb, whereas the other is possibly her mother's. Skin cells show similar mitochondrial DNA, though the results are inconclusive; the evidence wouldn't hold up in court. The key from the tool box is much more promising – both the front and back of the key have got smudged prints evident, which match reasonably well to Mrs Nadia Stoker, Angela's grandmother. I ran a check on her background – she has a previous conviction of falsifying her daughter-in-law's passport application, filed over thirty years ago. It appears that Mrs Sabina Stoker and her husband had an arranged marriage, which is unusual. The surname 'Stoker' wouldn't normally suggest to me that the original families had a similar cultural background. Sabina Stoker's birth certificate shows that she was actually only fifteen when she originally tried to enter this country as a married woman. The record states that Immigration officers became suspicious when she arrived in the country, checked the details on her falsified documentation, and refused her entry application at that time. Apparently, some Asian men have been known to take brides as young as twelve years old in their country of origin. Personally, I consider them still to be children – they need protection at that age."

"You need to remain emotionally detached where cultural traditions are concerned, Alexia. I must admit though, that this news of the grandmother's past has come as rather a shock. The case is now thrown wide open, but is starting to make a little more sense."

"Making more sense? In what way?" Alexia was finding it hard to view the case in a wider context – one that was not limited by scientific restraints.

"It's just an idea, but we will need to re-interview Mr and Mrs Stoker and find out what Angela's religious convictions were. I suppose there is the remote possibility that an arranged marriage was on the horizon for her. Can you ask Dan to call through to the passport office, and check for any visa applications in Angela's name – it's just a hunch, maybe nothing will come of it, but it's still worth checking."

"Yes, will do."

"Have you checked the girl's diary yet? I passed it to you for a woman's perspective on how the young female mind works. I'm here in hospital with Mr Michael and his mother at the moment. I've got a few questions I want to ask Mrs Michael, and then I'll head back to base. Luke Michael is still in a drug-induced coma, so he won't be able to talk to us for a few days, if at all."

"No, not really, I must confess. I skimmed through it,

and dusted it for prints, but that's about all. Quite a few references to spending time with the Angel, but not much else caught my attention. I'll give it a much closer look this afternoon. It feels like a real invasion of her privacy. I still remember how much I hated my mother when, as a thirteen year old girl, I caught her sitting on my bed reading through all of my private thoughts – an absolute humiliation! The experience scarred me emotionally, so much so, that I have never written anything private in a diary since then."

"You'll have to put all your personal history to one side, Alexia, and focus on the fact that the poor girl we are representing was plucked, partially clothed, from the sea, and has suffered the indignity of being photographed and cut open, with all her internal organs exposed, during a post-mortem examination with a total stranger. We owe it to her to follow any clues she has left us."

"Point taken," she replied. "I'm not quite myself today, as you're aware. It's a struggle to stay awake..."

"Hmm. Keep a grip on it kiddo! Going back to the diary content, Lauren Bale mentioned that her friend, Emma Waldron had referred to Mr Michael as 'Angel' when we interviewed her earlier in the week. Maybe there was some schoolgirl rivalry for Mr Michael's attention between Angela and Emma."

"Didn't she deny knowing Angela?"

"Kids tell lies, remember. I'll bring her and her mother in again for further questioning when I get back."

"There are some other results that I wanted to discuss with you, Steve."

"Fire away, kiddo."

"It's about the watch that was found in the cave, and fingerprints on Luke Michael's car steering wheel and boot lock. Angela's prints were on the watch-face, however, the strap revealed another set of yet unidentifiable, smudged prints. Nikki is trying to lift further DNA samples from it, in order to run a DNAboost profile; this should amplify and separate even the most miniscule quantities of genetic material on the strap. Judging from the combination of prints, we can assume that somebody forcibly removed the watch from Angela's wrist, and dropped it down the crevice in the cave by accident, before trying to lever it out again. This was possibly done post mortem. Presumably the majority of her clothes were removed in the cave at the same time. We need to scale-up the search for her school skirt and shoes. Her mother said these were all labelled with her name.

"Agreed."

"The hair on the blouse, that Lauren Bale was wearing, was definitely Angela's. The split cuticle shows that it was taken from a body after death. Other similar hairs were found at the cave mouth, so she was definitely dead before she entered the water. Scuff marks show that she was probably thrown into the water from that location."

"Good stuff, Alexia," replied Steve. "What were you going to tell me about the car?"

"We haven't got all of the results back yet, but we can definitely place another driver behind the wheel on the car's last journey – it was Steffan Locke, the chap that Jamie identified as one of the regular diving club members from images you showed him on your computer laptop. I've already checked Locke's records – he doesn't have a driving licence or valid insurance, so we definitely have grounds to bring him in for questioning."

"That's a really excellent lead. Can you get someone onto Locke for me please, in my absence? I'll phone through to the office, to confirm the arrangements when I leave this place, but at the moment, I'm in trouble with the old battle-axe that runs this ward. She's moaning, tut-tutting at me, and audibly tapping her feet on the floor, just like a bad-tempered brat! She doesn't appear to be able to communicate properly, so what hope have the patients got in this place? It transpires that you're not allowed to use mobiles here at all – I saw the explanation written on a sign in the corridor. Apparently, the signals from mobile phones interfere with the hospital electronic monitoring equipment. I figured it's more important to solve a murder than to avoid annoying a few nurses! Anyway, I'm sorry. I really shouldn't be ranting about it to you," he sighed.

"Don't worry about it Steve – we all have days when everything somebody says seems to wind us up. I suggest you step outside, grab some fresh air, and try to relax a little. The nurse is only trying to do her job – just like we're trying to do ours."

"You're right of course. I guess I'm just a little tetchy today. I'm really baffled by the emotionless detachment with which the hospital ward staff have been treating this frail old lady, who's only desire is to help her son to survive." He paused for a few seconds, to collect his thoughts. "Sorry

Alexia, where were we before I got side-tracked?"

"Steffan Locke."

"Oh yes, the delightful Mr Locke. We've charged him with grievous bodily harm on several previous occasions, but we haven't yet managed to secure a conviction. He had a really good lawyer that managed to clear his client on minor technicalities – the same lawyer that's representing Lauren Bale's interests."

"We can confirm that Steffan's fingerprints are all over the boot lock area of Luke Michael's car, as well as on the steering wheel," she added. "We're still awaiting results of the tissue samples found wedged in the car bumper. They should be back with us later today. The lab has been working twenty-four-seven on this case."

"Great. I owe you one for this."

"Let's make it a date then," blurted Alexia, surprising herself at the bluntness of her remark. "I could do to try out the new Vietnamese restaurant that opened last week. I've heard it's excellent, and besides, it's just round the corner from your place, so I can collect you if you wish. Oh, and don't worry, I'll be on soft-drinks all night." She paused briefly, hoping for a response. "How about we book for tonight, at around eight-thirty?"

"That sounds good to me. I didn't think you'd ever pluck up the courage to ask. Can I take it that you've got your car back then?" Steve asked.

"I sure have. I flashed my ID card (as you suggested), when I paid the bill, and they apologised profusely for the delay – they even offered me a free M.O.T. for next month, as a goodwill gesture."

CHAPTER NINE

"How are your pox then Sam?" Robyn tried her best to sound concerned and sympathetic to her friend's chickenpox predicament, when Sam excitedly intercepted the call Robyn made to Brett's mobile phone. She had waited five days after their last meeting before phoning the Stryder household, hoping that Brett would be eager-enough to have made contact with her instead. She could concentrate on very little other than fantasising at the thought of being asked out on another date by the tall, perfectly-tanned, fun-loving, charismatic Antipodean teenager. The suspense was becoming unbearable for her.

"They're itchy, but improving, thanks. I've had to paint pink calamine lotion on each of the spots, twice per day, every day this week – it smells rank! I'm determined not to leave the house until they've completely disappeared from my face and scalp, just in case anyone sees me like this. Mum reckons I should be well enough to be able to return to school again on Monday, unfortunately, so I'm making the most of my last few days of freedom. Actually, to be quite honest with you, I'm bored most of the time, unless my cousin Brett is here. He's got so many fascinating stories to tell, since his last stay here with us. Anyway, I heard he went out with you on Monday night, you lucky thing. I think he's so cool; what about you?"

"Yes, I thought so too. I just love that Aussie accent of his; it makes me go weak at the knees," she replied. "I'm a bit worried though, 'cos I haven't heard from him at all since Monday night. Has he mentioned anything to anyone about me?"

"All I know is that he got home really late, after getting lost in the village, and was quite bad tempered when he finally arrived here, which is unusual for him. He was soaking wet, and threw most of his clothes straight into the washing machine, which woke me up when it started spinning. He didn't say much to anyone about it."

"Oh!" Robyn replied. Her voice couldn't mask the disappointed. "I thought we got on really well – I thought he liked me. I hope it's not me that annoyed him."

"Don't ask me what's going on – it's really none of my business. One thing he did mention, though, is that he had to help break up a fight between Jamie and a man on the beach, just before he walked you home. He said he passed there again, on the way back from your place, and saw the same guy loitering with another man who was wearing a wet-suit, so he legged it, hoping that he wasn't spotted. Apparently, that's when he got so hopelessly lost."

"Has he told the police?" Robyn asked.

"No, I don't think so. Why would he need to? There are often drunks and homeless people that hang around on the benches down by the beach at night. My mum and Uncle Dave warned him to stay away from there, especially since he's a foreigner and an easy target for muggers. You certainly wouldn't catch me out there on my own after dark, but it doesn't seem to bother him – he prefers to be outdoors; he's a real action-man type."

"The man that attacked Jamie the other night was obviously targeting him for a reason. It's lucky that Brett intervened; it could have been a lot worse by the sound of things."

"Tell me more, what's been happening?" Sam asked. She didn't like being left out on anything involving her cousin.

"The guy was loitering outside of school, and apparently tried to follow Jamie home from school the next day."

"Why? What's going on?"

"I have absolutely no idea! Also, my sister seems to be in some sort of trouble at school, because of Mr Michael. Everything seems to revolve around the beach, on Monday night. Everyone is being really cagey about it, and won't tell me anything, yet they seem to expect me to give them answers to something I know nothing about," Robyn answered.

"I don't know what you're talking about, Robyn. Mr Michael, your dishy history teacher? What about him? Have I missed out on some juicy gossip?"

"Surely you know about him going missing? Rumours are all around school."

"What? You're joking! I saw something in the local newspaper on Wednesday, about a local man going missing, but hadn't associated it with anyone I would know, especially not Mr Michael from our school. He's always involved in lots of school activities and stuff; he's not the type to run away, or anything silly. Are you sure this is true? It's not just a silly wind-up, is it?"

"No, seriously, he hasn't been at school all week; we've had a supply teacher instead. It's not nearly as much fun in class as it usually is. Further more, my sister has been called over to the police station a few times this week, to answer questions, so there must be something unusual going on."

"I'll tell you what – why don't you come over here after you've finished your homework, and fill me in on what's been happening lately?"

"Homework? Not likely, it's Saturday today!"

"Really? Are you kidding me? I've seem to have lost track of time," Sam replied. "I am here on my own at the moment, so maybe you'd like to come over, anyway? I could do with some company, and anyway, with a bit of luck, Brett will be here soon, so you'll be able to chat to him too. He and Uncle Dave nipped into town, about an hour ago, shopping for souvenirs to take back home."

"I don't think I'll be allowed to come to your house until you've got rid of the chickenpox. Mum doesn't want me to catch it, since I was so poorly with it when I was a toddler," replied Robyn.

"You know that's rubbish, don't you, Robyn? You usually only get it once, and then you're immune to it for the rest of your life. My doctor said that I should only be infectious for a week after the rash appears, and I've already passed that stage. The virus takes between two and three weeks to incubate, so most of my friends might already have it."

"That's so kind of you to spread it around! So what are the early symptoms we should be looking out for?"

"I first knew about it when I started off feeling hot and had headaches at school, remember? The nurse in the medical room sent me home after I showed her the spots on the back of my neck. They were starting to appear on my front as well, but I wouldn't show her those, obviously."

"What about Brett, has he got it yet?"

"No, he's not likely to either. Uncle Dave told me that their whole family has already had it; they caught it years ago, when Brett was very young."

"That's one consolation, I suppose."

"Are you coming over then? I need to catch up on gossip."

"I'd better not, just now, at least until I've spoken to mum about it. She's out with Lauren again at the moment. It's all very 'hush-hush' so I don't know what they're doing, other than that they're meeting a chap called Mr Standish."

"I think I understand your reasons, I'll see you at school on Monday, if I don't see you beforehand," Sam replied. Her tone of voice reflected her disappointment at being left alone, bereft of her friend's company for yet another day.

"Will you let Brett know I called?" Robyn asked, hopefully.

"You can tell him yourself. He's just walked through the front door," replied Sam, as she handed the mobile phone to her cousin. Robyn felt her pulse rate speeding up as she awaited the sound of his voice again.

CHAPTER TEN

"Lexi, it's him, the man who attacked me! He's here – do something, help us quickly," said the anxious voice at the end of the phone.

Alexia rolled over, to switch the bedside light on, and checked the time on her clock-radio. It was nearly three-thirty in the morning. "Jamie, is that you? What's wrong? Can you speak up a little? I can barely hear what you're saying."

"I can't, sis, he'll hear me," Jamie whispered.

"Where are you? What's happening?"

"I'm at home, behind the downstairs cloakroom door. Mum and dad are still asleep in bed upstairs, I tried to wake them, but they ignored me. I thought I heard a window break in the kitchen, and crept downstairs to investigate it as soon as Sooty started barking and snarling. She's stretched out on the floor at the bottom of the stairs, she isn't moving; I hope he hasn't killed her. I can't go and check, because I'm blocked in here. I can see the man through the crack between this door and the frame – he's searching the drawers in the living room at the moment. Please hurry before he finds us! This is really urgent."

Alexia leapt out of bed. She could feel her pulse racing. "I'm straight on to it Jamie. I'll radio an emergency call directly through to the local police station. Stay where you are, and keep the mobile phone very close to your ear, so that my responses to you can't be overheard. You should speak only if I ask you a direct question, unless you feel threatened, or something else happens that you urgently need to tell me about." There was a lengthy pause, as Alexia radioed the details to her colleagues, and called Steve at home, using her landline. She attempted to dress herself one-handedly, whilst holding her mobile phone close to her ear with her free hand, so that she could keep communicating with her young brother. "Someone will be there with you in a few minutes, Jamie. I'm on my way as well. Take care bro', and try to keep as still as you possibly can, so that you don't draw attention to yourself. Agreed?"

"Yes, Lexi, but please hurry, before something happens to us."

"Trust me. I'll be there in less than five minutes. I'll let myself in through the conservatory door. Watch out for me, and keep calm, I'll come out from behind the curtains if I'm first on the scene. Don't be afraid."

Alexia knew that the journey would take considerably longer than five minutes to reach the Jackson house, and that the intruder could well have an accomplice acting as a lookout. She was aware that she would be deliberately placing herself in danger of increased vulnerability to any attack, until her colleagues arrived at the house. Her instinct was to protect her family at all costs, irrespective of DC Steve Turnbull's advice to leave any confrontation to the uniformed officers. Memories of the burglar who caused her grandfather's unnecessary death flooded back to her. She was furious, rather than being frightened by the situation, and was not about to allow any other member of her family to suffer the same fate, even if her actions caused her to lose her job. The adrenaline surging through her body heightened her self-confidence; she felt invincible, ready to place her own life on the line for the people she loved.

As she neared the house, she spotted blue lights flashing in the distance from her rear view mirror – she predicted that they would arrive within a minute of her own dramatic entry. There were no sirens sounding, the police officers obviously planned to capture the perpetrator in action. Her own thoughts were very different – she needed to flush the intruder out of the house as quickly as possible. "Jamie, are you safe?"

"I am at the moment. He's still downstairs, by the front door. I think he is texting someone from his mobile phone, but I can't see him very well at the moment, just the back of his coat. He took something out of dad's briefcase and put it in his ..." the conversation ended abruptly, as another person forcibly slammed the partly open cloakroom door onto Jamie, causing him to scream loudly and fall to the floor.

Alexia dropped her mobile onto the passenger seat,

and noisily brought her car to a halt, by skidding on the Jackson's gravel-covered driveway, in an attempt to draw the attacker away from her brother. Uniformed officers drew up beside her, and, without hesitation, made a forced entry to the house.

Jamie's mobile phone conversation, and background activity sounds had been constantly monitored via a radio link initiated before Alexia left her apartment. Steve leapt from his car, and physically restrained Alexia on the driveway of the house, until the two intruders were apprehended, arrested, and led outside, handcuffed. "Your family need you in one piece, kiddo. It's too risky to let you in on the action when you're this emotionally involved," he said, as he released his grip on her arms.

The bedroom lights now glowed from her mum's bedroom. Her step-dad, Mark, could be seen peeping through a gap in the curtains, obviously startled by the commotion both inside and outside of his home. "Jamie, I need to see my Jamie! I need to know he's alright," screamed Alexia, as she raced away from Steve. She found him crouched over his beloved dog, Sooty, oblivious to his own injuries. "Call an ambulance, quickly please mum," she shouted to the sleepy figure, who was now slowly walking down the stairs, dressed in a floral towelling dressing gown and furry slippers. "We'll need a police vet as well – I'll phone that one through myself, whilst you're calling the ambulance. Luckily, Sooty is still breathing, but we don't know what's happened to her. She's not moving."

Steve was still talking into his radio as he entered

through the front door, which was now precariously hanging from its hinges. He located Mr and Mrs Jackson, and ushered them into the living room. He briefly isolated them by closing the door behind him, as he remained in the entrance hall, thus avoiding his conversation with his colleagues being overheard. "Hey Dan, that's a great result, well done. Be sure to leave them in a draughty cell overnight, as soon as you and Dave have booked them in to the system. They can both stew a little until a sensible hour in the morning before we interview and charge them. That will give Miss Stermont's department time to collect any forensic evidence from the scene, and maybe even enough time to run comparison tests on the bottle of liquid that you found concealed in Mr Standish's pocket, against that which we recovered from Mr Michael's car boot. The distinctive labelling on both bottles appear to be similar, so I'm banking on them being from the same source, particularly since we now have a drowsy, immobilised dog as evidence. Darren, could you stay with Alexia and Jamie until the ambulance arrives, please. Take a statement of events, if the lad is capable."

"Mr Standish, did you say?" Dan asked Steve. "Mr Dean Standish, the lawyer?"

"Yes, that's right. The other chap we've captured tonight is his client, the notorious Steffan Locke, who we'd already issued an arrest warrant for. Locke's fingerprints matched those on the Ford Mondeo that was recovered from the bottom of the cliff last week, and I daresay that Dean Standish is the beach assailant from Monday evening. Jamie has already helped us to produce a photo fit image of his assailant, and will almost certainly be able to pick him out from an identity parade line-up, back at the station, as soon as we get it organised. We can't rely on his confirmation of identity based on a torch-lit image seen from behind a door during the break-in. Dean Standish is a competent lawyer, and would have no difficulty in having this dismissed as unreliable evidence, when the case goes before the judge. We will need to produce a robust case against him before we proceed to court. Mr Standish's fingerprints and shoe imprints will need to be cross-matched with those obtained from the inside of the discarded gloves and over shoe covers, recovered from the car crash vicinity, which have so far drawn a blank."

"That's interesting. No wonder Steffan Locke has managed to escape justice for so long, his lawyer has an excellent understanding on the limitations of forensic techniques that can stand up in court, and can manipulate a jury in his favour. I'll get his fingerprint images and a blood sample over to Miss Stermont's lab, for the attention of whoever is heading up the night service team, as a matter of urgency."

"I'll wait a couple of hours before waking Chief Inspector Lansing; this will make her day, even though it is a Sunday! If you put the blues and twos on when you get near to the police station, you'll almost certainly wake-up the local population and attract the attention of that irritating newspaper journalist who lives nearby; this could make the morning headlines – accidentally, of course. This is probably our best coup for weeks," added Steve.

"I'll do my best. There's nothing like blowing our own trumpets, eh? I can visualise the headlines now, 'Prominent lawyer arrested for burglary, and aggravated assault of a child.' I can tell you'll enjoy taking this one to court."

Steve re-opened the door to the living room, and found Mrs Jackson fast asleep again on the sofa. Mr Jackson appeared dazed, and disorientated. "I can't understand this," he said, "we only had one small glass of port last night, as usual, before going to bed. I can honestly say that I've never experienced this effect before. We keep the port in a decanter, so maybe it's gone off. I feel so very ashamed that we weren't awake to help our Jamie and Sooty when they needed us. Tell me, what actually happened here tonight?"

"We're still trying to piece things together, Dr Jackson, and will have a much clearer idea very soon. What we do know, however, is that Jamie claims that one of the men who broke into your house is the same man who attacked him on the beach last week. He mentioned during our interview earlier this week that he accidentally dropped his keys as he ran home from her house, and that he was too afraid to stop and pick them up."

"I think he's been using the spare key that we hide in the shed,' Dr Jackson replied.

"I'll check that out with him. Jamie also complained that the man from the beach is the same as who attempted to follow him home from school. I'm sure you'll agree that it is highly likely that these are connected events."

"Why do you think the intruder is interested in Jamie? It appears he was looking for something particular, rather than burgling our house, since the television, and computer have not been touched. As far as I know, nobody came in our bedroom, so they weren't after jewellery or anything of that nature."

"We heard Jamie say, over the radio, that the intruder took something from your briefcase. Can you check that please?"

"My documents and fossil samples are still here, but it does look as if my camera has been opened – yes – the memory card is missing."

"What is likely to be on it that is worth breaking into a house for?"

"There's nothing that I can think of. I tend to take photos of rock structures, and large fossils, which I use in my lectures. Many are from this local area."

"Do they contain people?"

"Sometimes, but I edit those out, normally. Having said that, a couple of weeks ago Jamie took a lovely photo for me, featuring a group of scuba divers. There was an incredible sunset which acted as a backdrop to the sea, which was lit up by their helmet lights. You can see the seaweed and silhouettes of fish quite clearly, interspersed with bubbles from the oxygen tanks. It looks magical."

"Did anyone notice him?"

"Probably, since he said there were a few people hanging around in the cave – he said he could see the glow from a fire, but not much else. Anyway, what does this have to do with the break in?"

"We'll have to retrieve your memory card, just to check."

"That's not really a problem. I upload my photos to my computer each week. I last did that a few days ago – I'll show you what's on there, if you like."

"Excellent. I'll need to copy the data files onto a CD. Our technicians will be able to enhance your images back in the lab; they could prove to be valuable evidence in an ongoing inquiry."

"What inquiry?"

"I'm sorry, but I'm not at liberty to discuss it at this stage; it could jeopardise our evidence for court," said Steve, embarrassed that he had mentioned it at all. "I'm sure you'll get an overview from the news this week."

"Ah, the blue lights suggest the paramedics have arrived for your son. He's the hero of the moment. Without his help, the outcome could have been considerably worse, taking into account the history of one of the intruders that we have apprehended here. He's taken a nasty blow to his head and shoulder, but hopefully he'll be okay."

"What about our Alsatian?"

"Your dog appears to be awake and breathing, but unable to move her muscles. We suspect that she may have been heavily sedated, or injected with a muscle relaxant. A police vet will arrive soon, to check her over."

CHAPTER ELEVEN

"You're a star, Lorne, thanks for that. I'll let Miss Stermont have the good news as soon as she arrives. She'll definitely need to be involved in taking responsibility for delivering the complicated forensic stuff, and fielding some of the inevitable awkward questions at the re-scheduled news conference tomorrow." Steve punched the air, with a glory salute, hardly able to contain his excitement, and promptly spilt his mug of coffee down the front of his newly dry-cleaned suit. He delighted at the fact that forensic evidence placed Standish and Locke at the location where Mr Michael's car was mysteriously launched over the cliff, as well as at the Stoker's house.

"We've worked non-stop during the night to work-up the evidence for this case, and have a few more results that might be of interest to you," added Lorne, keen to impress anyone who had the time and patience to listen to him. "Liam has authorised me to discuss the case results with you, now that the report has been finalised, so I'm not undermining Miss Stermont's authority."

"Let me have it then," replied Steve.

"I assisted Liam with the toxicology analysis, comparing the bottles of Rohypnol, using a gas chromatograph. The chromatograms are a hundred percent match, so they obviously came from the same source batch. There are also traces of the same drug in the dog's blood sample, taken by the vet last night, and in a blood sample provided from King's College hospital, taken from a Mr Luke Michael. What we don't yet know, is how it was administered to the dog. Was there a syringe, or a food bowl available to bag-up and sample?"

"I'm not sure. Alexia and a female police officer are still at the house, so I'll contact them shortly. Regarding Mr Michael, Rohypnol probably saved his life."

"How do you mean?"

"With a harpoon spear imbedded in his back, I would have expected him to have died from rapid blood loss; however, with a muscle relaxant in his circulatory system his heart might have been pumping the blood much slower than normal, heightening his chance of survival. I'm sure Alexia will lecture me on the science behind the theory, but does it sound plausible to you?"

"Yes, it sounds reasonable, but that's more Lyndsay's area of expertise. I can't give you an informed opinion, I'm afraid."

"That's okay. What else were you going to tell me?" Steve asked.

"Traces of Iron Sulphide and other grits from the soles of Dean Standish's shoes matched his shoe prints to those found on, and electrostatically lifted from, the limestone rock boulders located near to the cave entrance, as well as on the inside of the overshoe covers, which were discarded at the cliff top crime scene. The shoe covers and latex gloves are from the same manufacturer as those found at Mr Stoker's house during our search, and also at his place of work, Gale's Garage, just up the road from here."

"Gale's Garage you say? That's interesting," Steve commented.

"In what way? Have I missed out on something?"

"It's just a case of bringing all the facts together, which is why we've teamed up on this case. Everything is fitting into place very nicely. We already know that Standish, Locke and Stoker knew each other very well on a social basis – as Adam revealed by using digital enhancement of Mr Jackson's photos, taken by his son, Jamie, on the night that Mr Michael's attempted murder took place. It appears that it was this photographic evidence of the three scuba diving friends hunting their human prey that Dean Standish was so keen to recover from the Jackson's house during the early hours of this morning. He'll no doubt confess to this when we show him the photo, and try to strike some sort of plea bargain. I can't wait to see him squirm!" Steve chuckled to himself, whilst spinning around on his office swivel chair, excited by the department's success. He enjoyed the challenge of tying up the loose ends of a case, and ultimately dropping the laden report on his boss's desk, ready for trial proceedings to be initiated. With Alexia at his side, as an expert witness, the prosecution rarely faltered.

The attack on Luke Michael was clearly a well-planned revenge attack for the hit-and-run accident, involving Mr Stoker's daughter, Angela, which led to her eventual death, as she toppled over the crumbling edge of the cliff top, fatally fracturing her skull on the rocks below. The sheer edge of the cliff skirted by deep water during high tide could have carried the teenager's blood-covered body out to sea, though DC Steve Turnbull was concerned that this didn't explain how Lauren Bale was found wearing Angela's school blouse, which was not blood-stained or torn, on the Tuesday morning, five days after Angela was reported missing. He asked Lorne if the forensic report relating to analysis of the blouse had revealed any further clues.

"That's the funny thing, Steve. It wasn't Angela's blouse at all – it is the wrong size – it is one size smaller than the blouses we checked at the Stoker's house, and wouldn't have fit the body that we have in the morgue. The only epithelial cells, with the exception of one strand of Angela Stoker's hair, removed after she had died, belong to Lauren Bale, Emma Waldron and Alasdair Stoker, Angela's father. We can discount Lauren, since she was actually wearing the item of clothing; the blouse appears to be Emma's, with a replacement name label, sewn in by Mr Stoker. His DNA is on the cotton and the label itself. Emma possibly left her clothing at Angela's house during a sleep-over, or during an after school visit before they ceased to be friends."

"Perfect, that corroborates Lauren Bale's version of events, effectively eliminating her from our investigation, and explains why Jamie Jackson was attacked by Standish when he witnessed him rifling through one of the girls' school bags on the rocks that night."

"There's more, Steve – I was asked to check out Angela's possible arranged marriage status, by Dan – there is nothing to it. My search has revealed an interesting detail though; Dean Standish is her godfather. That might explain why he is involved in avenging her premature death."

"Mrs Michael phoned from hospital yesterday, to advise that her son had awoken from the coma, and had a burning desire to 'come clean' about his car accident. He made a statement from his hospital bed, to the Metropolitan Police Officers, confessing to running into an unknown schoolgirl with his car on the day he failed to report for work at school. He claims he didn't initially know who, or what, he had hit, as he briefly looked away from the road ahead and leaned down to change a CD in his car stereo. He remembers his nearside front wheel hitting an object, and jarring the steering wheel from his hand. At that point, he looked at his rear-view mirror; revealing the image of the crumpled body of a school girl, lying straddled across the road and the grass verge. He said he drove a little further along the road – parking the car safely in a lay-by before returning to the scene on foot. By that time, he claims that there was nobody remaining at the roadside, therefore assuming the girl was not too badly injured, and had continued walking to school He admitted irresponsibly driving away in panic, to avoid being breathalysed at the scene of the accident, as witnessed by the village postman. He then washed all visible evidence from his vehicle in the carwash at a Gale's Garage in Lychford Green, rather than driving a blood-stained car to school."

"That's right. Our analysis show that the body tissue samples wedged under the car's front bumper are an absolute DNA match to Angela," Lorne confirmed.

"That's a wonderful job! Tell you what, I'm just heading off home, and you must be at the end of your shift now, so do you fancy a celebratory pint and a bite of something to eat?"

"Sure I do. Where are you thinking of going?"

"I suggest we try 'The Lobster Pot' pub in Longbarrow village. Apparently they're serving a nice range of crab-meat sandwiches this week."

GLOSSARY OF
SCIENTIFIC TERMS

adrenaline: A hormone released into the bloodstream when a person experiences stress or fear.

algorithm: A method of manipulating data, to help solve a problem (often mathematical, when interpreting scientific data).

ammonite: An extinct species of marine animal (a mollusk), with a spiral shell. They lived predominantly in the Mesozoic era (65 to 248 million years ago)

analysis: Chemical or physical testing of a substance (when referred to in this forensic science context).

aroma: A smell.

asthma: A chronic medical condition characterised by difficulty in breathing. The cause is attributed to constriction of the bronchioles within the lungs. This can be effectively controlled by medication.

beta-test: Testing performed using a developmental (trial) version of the final product.

calcium carbonate: Chemical formula: $CaCO_3$
This is a compound which contains bonded calcium, carbon and oxygen atoms. Common rock forms of this mineral are chalk, and limestone.

capillary: The narrowest and thinnest-walled of the three types of blood vessel. Its diameter is slightly wider than a red blood cell. Capillary walls consist of a single layer of cells.

Ceramic: Clay-based objects, which have been heated to high temperatures, to alter their chemical structure.

chickenpox: A childhood disease caused by an air-borne herpes virus. This usually affects children under ten years old, who often then become immune to it for life.

chromatogram: The displayed image (by a printer output, or a computer screen) showing the results of an analysis performed using the chromatography technique.

chromatography: The analytical technique which is used to obtain the separation of a mixture of gases, liquids, or materials that have been dissolved in a solvent.

coma: A state of unconsciousness. The patient cannot be woken-up.

crevice: A narrow crack in a rock.

crustacean: A member of the class of arthropods – animals which have a hard, segmented external skeleton, including: crabs, lobsters, and shrimps.

DNA: This is an abbreviation for Deoxyribonucleic acid. These molecules carry genetic information. DNA fingerprinting techniques allow individuals to be identified from their unique sequences (their DNA profiles) of repeated sections of this molecule. DNA has a double helix structure.

essential oil: A fragrant plant extract oil, often used in flavourings or perfumes.

fluorescence: Substances which emit light (glows) when bombarded by radiation or light from another source.

forensics: Scientific evidence, to be used in a court of law.

fossil: Evidence of the remains of previously-existing

plants or animals which have been preserved in mineralised form in sedimentary rocks.

genetics: The study of how characteristics are passed from one generation to another in living organisms.

incubation: Providing heat and nutrients for an organism to develop.

infectious: Being capable of spreading a disease or infection.

inflammation: Swelling or redness which appears in the soft body tissue near to and around the source of infection.

infrared radiation: Part of the electromagnetic spectrum, where wavelengths are between the long wavelength region of visible radiation (700nm) and the microwave region. Infrared radiation cannot be seen by the naked eye.

inhaler: A hand-held medical device which allows the user to inhale a measured amount of powdered drug.

innards: Internal body organs.

iron oxide: Chemical formula: FeO
Iron oxide is a reddish brown solid, commonly known as rust, when seen as a coating on iron objects.

iron pyrite: Chemical formula: FeS_2
Iron sulphide is a shiny yellow-gold coloured solid, found naturally in metamorphic and igneous rocks, as well as in seams within sedimentary rock. It is commonly termed 'fool's gold'.

Jurassic period: Part of the Mesozoic era of geological time; 208-146 million years ago.

latent: Something that potentially might be present, but is not immediately obvious or easy to detect.

latex: A form of rubber.

limestone: A sedimentary carbonate rock, deposited on the ocean floor, resulting from marine organism's skeletal remains. Mineral composition is predominantly calcite ($CaCO_3$).

limpet: A marine snail with a conical shell. They adhere to rocks when not feeding.

luminescence: Light emission by an object, which is at a non-elevated temperature. This is a result of action on the object by light or other radiation, and does not necessarily cease when the original source of energy is removed.

microscopic: Too small to be seen by the naked eye.

mitochondria: An organelle within a cell, which is associated with energy transformation processes.

nucleus: A spherical or ovoid membrane-bound compartment within a cell, which contains the genetic material (DNA).

opacity: The limit to which something is light-obscuring, (how opaque it is).

organism: A living plant or animal.

oxidise: To undergo a chemical reaction with oxygen, to form an oxide. Oxidation can also mean the loss of electrons (same process as if losing them to oxygen).

ozone: The chemical formula is: O_3
Ozone is a highly reactive gas, with a distinctive odour. When in the Earth's upper atmosphere, it helps to protect the planet from ultraviolet rays, which are known to be a cause of skin cancer.

pallid: The term is often used to refer to something that lacks colour.

paramedic: Ambulance staff trained in life-saving

skills, including emergency care involving the use of intravenous medication.

patchouli oil: A fragrant essential oil, extracted from the leaves of Asiatic trees of genus Pogostemon. The oil is often used to make perfumes.

pathology: The study of the cause, nature and origin of disease, mainly associated with body tissue. A pathologist will be involved in examining a body to establish the cause of death.

Polythene: A polymer of the ethylene molecule, (it is also known as polyethylene). It is a versatile plastic with many industrial uses.

post-mortem: Occurring after death.

prosthetic: An artificial replacement for a body part.

radiate: Spread out in all directions from a central position. This is often associated with wave motion, or radiation (such as light or heat)

resonance: An amplified sound produced by vibration of an object.

sample: A small portion of a substance.

satellite: An object orbiting a planet or star.

secretion: A substance that is released from a cell.

spatter: A pattern of scattered drops, possibly caused by splashing, dropping or squirting a liquid.

spirogyra: Green freshwater multi-cellular alga. It is named after the spiral coils of chloroplasts.

sprain: A temporary joint injury caused by sudden twisting of the ligaments, which produces painful swelling.

torso: The upper part of the (human) body – the 'trunk' area, not including arms or head.

toxicology: The study of poisons, and their effects.

trait: A characteristic of a person.

trauma: An injury or wound to the body. This can also be used to describe a psychological injury caused by a sudden shock.

ultraviolet: The part of the electromagnetic spectrum with wavelengths shorter than those of visible light, but longer than x-rays.